SACRED

The Unwanted Series, Book III

C. M. NEWELL

SACRED, The Unwanted Series, Book III

An eBook Me Up Publication by arrangement with the author.

Copyright © 2022 by C. M. Newell

Cover Designer Maria Spada

Hard Cover Print ISBN: 978-0-9976836-8-4

Print ISBN: 978-0-9976836-7-7

eBook ISBN: 978-1-956049-09-1

CONTENT WARNINGS

Bullying Behavior
Death, Murder

To my father who taught me to be my own hero, since he has always been mine.

SACRED

TABLE OF CONTENTS

PART I

Chapter 1   3
Chapter 2   13
Chapter 3   27
Chapter 4   39
Chapter 5   47
Chapter 6   59

PART II

Chapter 7   73
Chapter 8   85
Chapter 9   91
Chapter 10   101
Chapter 11   113
Chapter 12   129
Chapter 13   143
Chapter 14   157
Chapter 15   167

PART III

Chapter 16   181
Chapter 17   195
Chapter 18   209
Chapter 19   219
Chapter 20   225
Chapter 21   233

PART IV

Chapter 22   245
Chapter 23   257

Chapter 24   267
Chapter 25   271

Author's Note   277
Acknowledgments   279
Also by C. M. Newell   281
About the Author   283

PART I

The cycle of the moon begins where it's desired; for it's the call and forward actions of a waxing moon.

~The Goddess

CHAPTER 1

Fiddling with my hands, dressed in my academic black robe, I feel like I'm dressed for a funeral, not graduation. My mind is wandering in the past. The absence of those gone and the changes for those who remain, me included—the future.

I've made it somewhat unscathed through my last year of high school in Chepstow, Massachusetts, all while becoming the Wiccan Queen of Edayri. Two parts of my life collided, and I came out scarred but stronger.

Headmaster Chin approaches the podium and clears her throat.

"Ladies and gentlemen, I now present to you the graduating class of Trinity Cross."

The breath I hold releases.

I mimic the joy on my classmates' faces. In celebration, I throw my graduation cap high into the sky. There is a ripple overhead before the bellow of thunder. Lightning streaks across the sky within seconds of another loud crack and boom. Light rain becomes a downpour with a third crack of thunder.

Boom!

So much for the lovely outdoor ceremony and the weather forecast of sunny skies.

The graduation caps and paper programs litter Trinity Cross High School grounds. I turn from my row and follow my classmates to meet our friends and family in the stands placed in a square around the campus greenway. I wave to Sabine, Eoin, Quinn, Cross, Thaxam (under substantial glamor), and my Uncle Evan in the metal riser seats on the opposite side of the quad. They are looking up and around, faces full of concern. Except for Evan, whose eyes are closed, and head tilted. Not paying attention, I run into the backside of Coral.

"Sorry," I mumble, but she doesn't acknowledge me because she is looking straight up. A purplish-blue hue moves and swirls fast in the now clouded sky.

Loud voices are incoherent near me, no longer echoing with the cheers and well wishes of graduated classmates and their families. The sky crackles and reveals a kaleidoscopic pattern of symbols. They appear and disappear in the clouds.

Magick is humming like a vibration in my arms

and legs. A supercharge of power. I suspect, without looking down, my magick is revealing itself on my skin to everyone around me, the glowing patterns on my skin, and the crown that floats above my head. I panic before scoffing at myself as if anyone is paying attention to me with everything else happening around us. Regardless, I mentally pull it back in with a concentrated inhale. The storm is its beacon—a calling. I stand still, trying again to regain control of the power within my veins.

I'm losing my mind. This is only a storm. We're not in Edayri, where magick is standard. The weather in Chepstow, Massachusetts, at the end of May, is unpredictable. I remember the one time it snowed. I shake out my hands, grateful I can hide my magick from outsiders.

Rain isn't anything to get worked up about, right?

I walk to the side of Coral and pass her to find Sabine running toward us. Her red hair is no longer pinned back, but wild in the wind. Lightning strikes and smacks the ground, throwing me and scattering those nearby. I shake my head hard to rid the clouded vision, along with the muffled sound of ringing in my ears. But the burning smell invades my nose and makes me choke.

I kick my feet at the grass that is smoldering closest to me. Black burned patches of grass surround the quad. Black smoke surrounds me. Vertigo strikes hard, and I roll onto my hands and knees. I push down my overwhelming need to heave as I stumble to stand.

People are running, and the first thing I hear is Sabine's muffled scream of my name. Then a roar of an enormous wild cat? Everything is off balance. My hands are numb and shaking. I pop my jaw with an exaggerated drop of my chin, and sounds become clearer. I shield my eyes from the now pelting rain and see a dark fissure in the quad.

Phantoms.

I remember the Phantoms rising from the earth near MacKinnon Manor. Are they back?

No. They can't be.

The gate closed with the death of Mr. Boward. This rationale doesn't stop my mind from running wild, staring into the open wound in the ground of dark mud. My heart is thundering in my chest. Again, the roar of a cat echoes, followed by more screams. I buckle over to a sharp pain in my stomach. An additional pulse and pull with a new crack of lightning.

"Help! Help me!"

The shrill scream is nearest to me. It's Coral. I barely find her with the black graduation robe and her dark hair. Dark smoke concealing her only. It's her pale hands that I see first clutching into the side of the muddy ground, struggling to climb out. I focus on the bright blue sash of our school colors. On my knees I slide forward, and I stretch out.

"Grab my hand!"

A cramp tugs on my insides, but I keep my arm outstretched.

"I can't! Willow, please . . . Help me!" Coral cries.

My shoulder pops when I thrust my magick down my arm, into my hand. It pushes back, pain twisting and radiating throughout my body, a rejection. Black smoke rushes at me like a magickal whip, stinging me.

Yelling in my head, I command my magick to obey my intentions. We get tossed in the air together, limbs smacking and flying in a heap of mud; my back slams into the ridge of the sidewalk near the front office of the school.

"Ah!"

Stunned, I curl into myself. The pain is spreading through me, the sting the smoke. I can't breathe. I reach for my magick, finding its weak tether. I must pull it—force it.

Tick . . . tock.

"Willow? Hold on," Sabine says. The warmth of her magick flows into me and eases the sharp pain.

Sirens sound in the distance, and a few people are running toward us with umbrellas. I turn to Coral, who is lying prone with her hands over her face.

"Can you move?" I ask her as a muscle in my back tightens.

She nods, and we move from our knees and scoot under the closest awning. Coral's parents rush to her the black smoke vanishes into the ground. Sabine is wet from head to toe, whereas Coral's parents are untouched by the rain with their umbrellas.

"We need to go. It isn't safe here. Cross and Quinn should have the SUV waiting for us."

"Thank you for your help," Coral's father says with a weak smile, watching me before he hugs Coral tight again. Her stepmother pats Coral on her back in a stiff, forced way.

With half-lidded eyes, she says, "I'm so glad you are both fine."

Despite her wrinkled forehead, I doubt her sincerity. Her voice is more penetrating than I expected and almost accusatory.

"I'm Vanessa, Coral's stepmother. I learned about Willow's father, your son's passing? Sorry for your loss."

She reaches for Sabine's hand, but Sabine keeps both her hands on my shoulders.

"Thank you. He was my son-in-law."

Sabine plasters on her political smile, and in one minute, we have said goodbye and passed under the arched front gates of Trinity Cross High School. This isn't how I thought I would exit high school for the last time, but then again, why would this day be typical?

My stomach twists with a new roar of thunder that claps in the distance. Sabine's face contorts. She senses it, too. The surrounding air is electric, and the hair on my arms rises and prickles. Both my and Sabine's magick flickers to the surface of our skin and it fades just as fast. Sabine steadies herself on a nearby car.

"You feel that?"

"Yes."

Quinn pulls up in the SUV. I shrug off the muddy graduation robe and get into the vehicle.

"Let's go!" Cross yells.

Quinn maneuvers through the parking lot. We're on the main road in less than a minute, passing the firetrucks and police who are arriving at the high school.

"That's one hell of a graduation, Willow," Cross laughs.

Despite the good nature of his comment, Sabine scowls. "Those patterns in the sky are Druid symbols."

Again, my stomach twists, and I lean over in my seat. Quinn's eyebrows furrow as he stares straight ahead.

"We all sense it. What is this?" I ask.

"I'm afraid this is the beginning of the Convergence. Esmund has hastened what we feared. I expected we'd have more time, years even. The legion council and Evan began preparing for—"

At the mention of Mr. Boward's name, my thought is of Rhydian. Is he okay? Does he realize what's going on? I hang onto the last moment we shared a kiss that made my toes curl and my stomach drop.

He left us—me; he left me.

I sigh before I swallow hard and focus on her mentioning Mr. Boward. He planned to kill me and so many others. In the end, I turned it on him, which resulted in his death instead. Rhydian's father's death . . . Rhydian must hate me. My heart squeezes in my chest, the familiar pain radiates through me, and my hands ball up into fists. Every time he enters my mind, I regret my actions in breaking the blood vow. His absence, another type of constant suffering.

My thoughts go wild in the vehicle despite Sabine talking about the next steps and her assumptions about what is happening. The Convergence is here, and again, my worlds are colliding. This is inevitable, right?

Quinn pulls into the drive of my father's house— my house. The protection enchantments surround the house. The lawn wavers as if surrounded by a bubble, a type of iridescent glow from the sun's rays escaping the clouds. I could never visibly distinguish them before. Does that mean anyone can see them? Is this magick visible to everyone?

We drive through them. My stomach releases, but the knot replaces with a pounding pulse in my head. I exhale and shake my hands from their tight grip. I look up to find Theon and Ax standing in the garage.

My immediate thought is: Where are Evan and Commander Eoin?

CHAPTER 2

When Theon and Ax enter the house from the garage, they hardly acknowledge us pulling in. Ax ducks so his horns don't catch on the door frame while entering the house. A blood demon is a sight you don't easily forget, considering how enormous he is.

Quinn touches the button on the roof of the SUV that closes the garage door.

"Well, this was fun."

Sabine gets out of the car and slams the door. The sound echoes. I gnash my teeth as I jump, still cold, wet, and muddy. I brush past her when we enter the house into the laundry room. Grabbing a towel, I wipe my face and wring my hair. Everything appears excessive, not only the rain and mud, but the surrounding air. I feel heavy. I take off my shoes with my toe.

Can't I have just one regular event in my life? I know the answer, watching Cross and Quinn toss each other towels.

Absolutely not.

Sabine waves her hand, and she dries her clothes as magick moves up her body. As magick reaches her hair, Cross whistles low. Her hair is turning white.

"Goddess, stop!" I shriek.

Sabine looks over her shoulder, the widening eyes as we watch her red hair turn white. She clutches her hands into fists, to stop the magick. But it doesn't completely stop what's already in motion. She now has stark white strands at her temple and crown. The once vibrant red is dull, mixed with white hair throughout. She resembles the part of my grandmother, now more than ever.

I'm not sure of the sound escaping my open mouth. Shock or amusement, but either way, both Quinn and Cross echo me.

Sabine squints her eyes at us before; she gives a grim smile because now we are all in a full-on belly laugh between me, Quinn, and Cross. Are we laughing or crying?

"You're laughing at me?"

"So, do you typically magick your hair color?" I ask.

The rumbles of laugher slowly die away.

Sabine replies, "An afterthought, but I've always had red hair. I'm going to have to concentrate on not using magick. Magick is not working correctly with these rifts." She throws her hands up. "I'm sure it's not safe to transport. We are not testing that out!"

"So, you know what this is? What did you call them, rifts? At graduation? The storm broke the earth apart . . . I had déjà vu from the Phantoms."

"Me too," Quinn replies. His eyes soften. He knows the part I relive. A shiver trails up my spine along with a squeeze and ache—Rhydian.

I depart for my room to shower and change out of the wet and muddy clothes.

Getting dressed, I bend forward, and my muscles strain and pinch. I twist side to side to surrender the weight and pressure of the events, but nothing pops or releases. There is no relief as I stretch. My magick is under the surface of my skin. Usually, my magick is bright and vibrant, but now my eyes strain to see the flow of patterns from my magick. The connected hum isn't strong, but it's there.

I look at myself in the mirror before leaving my room. I'm not noticeably changed on the outside, but on the inside, I grasp the boldness and courage I need to face the unknown. Downstairs, I overhear voices in the formal living room and gravitate toward them versus standing at the top of the stairs.

"Quinn, comms are still down," Cross says. He taps his wrist cuff, but nothing happens.

"Commander and Evan transported to Edayri, at the beginning of the rifts. I don't suggest we try. The ability to control magick is . . . Well, is clearly off," Quinn replies with a small smile toward Sabine and her now white streaks of hair.

"The Guardian wrist cuff is not working?" Sabine huffs. "This is unfortunate."

That doesn't mean all communication is absent. Holding my ruined phone, I hold up my finger and rush into father's office. Ax and Theon sit in the wing-backed chairs in front of the gas fireplace.

"What do you need?" Ax asks, joining me at the desk.

"Dad always had a backup cell phone," I say. Rumbling in the first drawer of his desk, which is full of pens and minor items. I find the cell phone, plug it in, and the boot-up begins.

"What are you doing?" Theon asks. When Sabine, Quinn and Cross join us in the office, I smirk.

"The twenty-first century magick of all teenagers. Let's text and get some information."

At least I hope this works. It beats sitting and doing nothing.

Theon rolls his eyes. "It's just a cell phone."

"Not just any cell phone. One magicked for non-regional and realm communication."

Quinn explains how Rhydian had magicked my phone number. It enabled me to talk and text my friends from either realm, no matter where I am physically.

"If I import my information onto this phone, it could work," I say to no one in particular. At least I can reach Emily and Marco and find out what's going on with these storms and rifts. The hair on the back of my neck rises and the sensation of electricity runs down my back. Possibly these are aftershocks of what happened in Edayri with the Phantoms.

"How long is it going to take?" Cross asks.

"I need to charge up this backup phone, and then I can transfer . . . It will take a bit of time."

Sabine is pacing back and forth in the office's doorway. I've never known Sabine to be impatient. But I don't blame her. I'm impatient too, but at least I have something keeping me less idle—a task, a plan.

Goddess, I hope this works.

Maybe.

Cross and Quinn sit in front of the long windows for a game of chess at the small table. Whereas Ax and Theon have taken their residence in the wing-backed chairs. Theon has a book in his hands, reading. Ax has leaned his head back and closed his eyes. He appears peaceful, the huge red demon with horns on top of his head. He seems out of place, and yet Duke is at his feet sleeping.

Time is slow sitting in my father's chair for a half-hour, watching the old phone blink while accepting all the data from my phone.

"How can you all just sit?" Sabine says.

Ax, with shut eyes, responds, "Do you have a better idea?"

Quinn responds, "We suspect the Commander and Evan are in Edayri coordinating efforts. You sense it, right? The rifts of magick moving like tectonic plates shifting here in the Terra realm, like a magickal earthquake?"

Theon's half-closed eyes reveal his exhaustion before he continues. "Evan told us to come here. So, we did. Brought back the Ford Escalade we drove."

Sabine stops pacing. "Willow, try to move something. Your magick is the strongest here, blessed by the Goddess, the Wiccan Queen. Do nothing to yourself or others directly, we learned that lesson." She twists her white hair around her finger, and Cross smirks.

"Why? This changes nothing."

Does it? I could help others if I could use my magick reliably with nothing strange happening.

My eyes gravitate to a small porcelain flower vase on the side table next to the wingback chairs.

Tick-tock.

The hum rises when I call to my magick. But it's off, not the soothing liquid flow that I usually receive in my veins. It's a staccato movement. The echo that only I hear isn't a hum, but like the static, you sometimes hear on the radio. I focus on the flow to calm it, and it gets a little smoother. Sabine and all of them are watching me. I slowly twist my steady hand and pick up the flower vase with the air surrounding it, to move it to the matching side table of the opposite wingback chair. The vase moves, hovers, and then floats between the two chairs. I sense the pulse, the interruption. I force the air before—

Boom.

"Dammit!"

"Well, one thing is for certain: we have magick, but it's unpredictable. Or . . ." Sabine says.

"Or what?" Cross asks.

"Magick is disappearing?"

Sabine's face drops, and her eyes shut as she looks away from me. Her shoulders shake a little, only I notice the bend in my stoic grandmother's back. My desire for an everyday life seems so long ago now. The idea of magick leaving isn't one I'm ready to take as truth. I'm used to who I am with magick and how it makes me feel strong, empowered, confident. Part of it ties me to my father and my mother. If it somehow disappears . . .

"It's possible, Willow," Sabine says, wholly composed now. Her emotions are in check. How can she do that? I want to yell and cry, but what would it solve?

A phone signal radiates in the room. Charging is complete, and notification beeps sound one after another. Sabine hovers over my shoulder.

"Who are ya going to text?" Cross asks.

Why is it my first instinct to check on Rhydian? He's made it clear he will not reach out to me, but it doesn't mean I stop caring. The twist and ache in my stomach, the pounding at my temples, is something I'm used to. There is a part of my brain that wars over respecting his decision and being angry at him because of the rejection that I feel from him needing space. Is it wrong to worry about him in this crazy storm?

I stare at the smartphone in my hands, and it makes a choice for me when a text message appears.

Eoin: *Do not use magick, do not transport. This is a broad public message.*

I read it out loud and text back.

Willow: *What is going on? Do you need Sabine and me in Edayri? Ax, Theon, Cross and Quinn are here too.*

Cross is now pacing back and forth in front of me. It is like we are awaiting news in the lobby of a hospital. The notification ping brings everyone's attention back to the phone.

Eoin: *No! Stay put. People are being lost in the magickal*

rifts. I cannot do my job if I worry about you. Stay put until it's safer.

I repeat the response.

Theon throws his hands in the air. Ax grunts before sitting.

"What are you thinking?" I ask Sabine and Quinn, standing in front of me.

She hugs her waist. "Guess we wait for now. You like the idea as much as I do. I don't know what we could walk into. We need to stay here."

Nodding in agreement, but even staying put doesn't mean I can't reach out or know what's going on. "I'm going to text my friends."

Sabine leaves with Ax and Theon to show them where the guest rooms are. Cross and Quinn stay and play more chess. I curl up in a chair that faces the window and stare at the phone in my hand.

I want to text Rhydian. Instead, I reach out to Emily.

Willow: *Em, are you okay? Daniel? Marco? Any news?*

Em: *We are at my house right now. Marco can't control his shifting, which, at least at my home, isn't problematic— for the moment.*

Willow: *That can't be good.*

Em: *No, it isn't, but at least we are shielding him from—*

A minute passes with no response.

Willow: *Em?*

Em: *Gotta go. Be safe. Check-in later.*

Willow: *Okay, you too.*

Duke is curled up at my feet, and I stroke his fur with my hanging foot as I stare at the empty screen. My fingers are working faster than my brain. I type a message to Rhydian.

Willow: *Are you okay? In Chepstow, at the house. Would you mind letting me know if you're okay?*

The message is delivered, and within only a few seconds it shows as read. I wait, chewing my fingernail. The read receipt stays static, no motion, or blinking cursor to show an active response is coming. Does he care about how I'm doing? Gah, I'm so selfish. I wonder if he's hurt or something? Before my mind takes the swan dive into the dark abyss of worse possibilities, the phone pings, alerting me to a new text message.

I wave off Cross's grunt.

Rhydian: *Yes. Crazy storms. Are you okay?*

He's asking about me. Me. I type back quickly.

Willow: *I'm okay. Magick isn't working right. The storm created chaos at graduation, including a massive hole in the school's quad.*

I wait for what seems like a few minutes, but it's only been thirty seconds. There isn't a response.

I type, *I miss you.* And it blinks back at me, mocking me. I delete it; I can't send it.

The phone buzzes in my hand. It's Rhydian. He's calling me! Quinn and Cross turn toward the sound. I look away. I should have called, but I'm a coward. My heart pounds, and I wait for the second buzz before I answer it.

"Hey," I say, but the voice that reaches my ears is not the one I am expecting.

It's Tullen. He's been with Rhydian since he left Edayri.

Before I hear what he is saying, I ask him to hold on for a minute. Hitting mute, I stand and walk out of the office, away from Quinn and Cross. I needed the voice to be Rhydian. Taking two calming breaths, holding in the tears that threaten to fall, I sit on the stairs.

"Hi, Tullen. Are you okay?" Hopefully, he doesn't hear the disappointment in my voice.

"Well, it's relative, but yes, we are fine. I'm waiting for orders from the Commander and right now it is to stay put. We haven't heard yet from anyone else."

I'm the first.

"Where are you? Are you in Edayri or still—"

"Actually, we are in Tulsa, Oklahoma. We were making our way out of town when the storms began here too, so we're at a restaurant waiting it out," Tullen says.

"Tullen, is Rhydian? I just, yeah, I—"

"He's better, but it's a process. Be patient with him and me," Tullen says.

"With you?"

"I have this notion that I deserted you. I know I didn't, but the global storms have me second guessing everything at the moment."

"Sabine suspects it's the Convergence, too. Do you think so?"

Tullen is reticent and then he continues. "I think so, yes. Mr. Boward accelerated it, and I think it's started. The realms are unstable, so magick is volatile, transporting isn't an option right now."

I swallow, and my throat is dry.

"Tullen, you didn't desert me," I say. After all, I asked him to take care of Rhydian and go with him.

"Thank you for that. If you hear from Quinn or Cross, can you tell them we'll be in touch as soon as we can?"

My heart beats faster. "Does that mean you're heading toward Chepstow? Quinn and Cross are here with me."

"No, Rhydian has another destination first. I can't tell you more, but we'll be there before you know it."

My mouth is braver than my brain. "Can I speak with Rhydian? Is he there?" My heart is loud in my ears. I hear a muffled sound of a hand over the phone. "Tullen? Are you there?" The instant sinking sensation in my stomach tells me that Rhydian is next to him.

"Willow, I need to let you go. Rhydian will call you when he can, okay? Be well."

The call ends too soon.

I stare at the phone, willing it to ring again, but it doesn't. I toss it on the foyer table before I walk back into the office.

"How is he? Or more to the point, are you okay?" Quinn asks.

I don't know if they heard much of the conversation. I try my best to smile and pull off the outer appearance of being fine, even though I'm anything but. It's nice that they are here. I don't like to be alone in this big house.

"I'm the same—no better, no worse. And they are okay. Supposedly, he'll call me when he can, but I suspect that won't be for a while. It was Tullen that I was talking with."

"I figured as much." Quinn walks to me and holds my shoulders. "I'm sorry that he left."

Cross is studying the sky from the windows. "Right now, we need to keep our heads about ourselves."

Can I do that? Keep my head when it comes to magick and to Rhydian?

Tick-tock.

CHAPTER 3

The doorbell echoes through the house. I rush from my bedroom to the top of the stairs, where I find Daniel holding a box with a red ribbon. He's smiling and politely talking with Sabine. His face lights up when he sees me, and despite his polite smile, the corners of his mouth pull as if he can smile more. I laugh and run down the stairs. Happy for the freedom from my insane boredom of this crazy day.

"What are you doing here?" I ask.

Sabine scolds me playfully, "Is that any way to greet a friend who's come to see you?"

Daniel stands a little straighter before he says, "Actually, I was asking your grandmother to get you out of the house."

I look from Sabine to Daniel and back to Sabine.

"Really? You're okay with me going out with the storms?"

I say storms, but the weather has receded around Chepstow. Storms now are code for the Convergence. I assumed we were under house arrest until we got further news from Eoin.

"Why not? Our plans following graduation were disrupted, so you might as well enjoy some time with your friends. Just be careful and stay close to town." Sabine walks away.

I point to the box in Daniel's hands. "What do you have there?"

He hands me the box. It has some weight to it.

"Just a little something I thought you would enjoy. Not every day we graduate from high school." His face, although happy, is a mask. He wasn't at graduation. I know why, but it still pulls at my heart when I think about it.

"May I open it now?"

"Ah, absolutely." He stands back and watches as I pull the ribbon and lift the delicate top of the box. Moving the tissue paper, I find a journal with my name engraved.

"Daniel, this is beautiful."

My fingers touch the smooth leather and trace the indentations that spell my name. I set the box on the foyer table. I open the journal. The spine cracks and moans as I turn the pages to the thick, blank paper.

"Drawing pencils are at the bottom of the box."

I want to say more, but I don't. I touch the smooth pages.

"It's a sketchpad and a journal. I figure it might be a good idea for you to get your thoughts down and out of your head. I remember when you used to draw during Junior year. You loved it."

It's the most thoughtful gift I've received. He's right. To get these rumbling thoughts out of my head. I lay the sketchbook next to the box. Stepping into Daniel, I hug him.

"Thank you."

Two brief words say so much and so little, for the boy who I once loved.

"Willow, let's get out of the house. Go to A Cup of Joe's? Anything is better than seeing you mope."

"I'm not moping. Well, not a lot anyway."

His eyes are assessing. And I can't help but laugh. He taps me playfully on the shoulder.

"Okay, fine. Let's go to A Cup of Joe's and catchup."

"How about you drive."

I nod my head to the back of the house. Daniel, being the car guy he is, can't resist breaking into a big grin. I could have sworn I overheard him say, "Hells yeah!" In the garage, he carefully assesses the six bays with various cars, including mine, that my father gave me. Daniel walks over to the dark gray

Audi R8 and claps his hands together and rubs them vigorously.

"Okay, fine."

I grab the keys off the key hook by the front door and toss them over to him.

Getting in the car, it still has the new car smell. His grin is so wide it's hard not to laugh as I lean back into the curve of the seat. He's being careful as we slip out of the neighborhood. On the main road, he puts the pedal to the metal, and we accelerate with the easy speed of the car.

I roll down the window part way and the weight of the day lifts despite all the unknowns. The fresh air of new blooms in Massachusetts fills the car. Summer is almost here.

"So, what do you think of the car?"

"I think I need to take it further than A Cup of Joe's, like we need to drive all around. And maybe even find some nice straightaways."

It's easy hanging out with Daniel. He's how I remember him when we were dating, more like his old self, more comfortable in his own skin. My heart warms at his smile and his bright eyes. Not that long ago that he died right in front of me. Then Lucy brought him back as an einherjar soldier. It was Lucy's first time using her magick as a half valkyrie, but she did it with Emily's help as a full and trained valkyrie. However, it didn't turn out the way Lucy wanted for her boyfriend. This only drove them further apart. He's now under Emily's tutelage, since Lucy still doesn't want any part of her magickal heritage.

As he drives, I stare out the window. We enter the town center and see people shopping and continuing on as normal in the twilight of evening. I'm not sure what I expected, but business as usual was not it. It was as if nothing out of the normal occurred earlier today, despite the global news reporting it all.

"Strange, huh?"

I turn to Daniel. "What's strange?"

"How the world carries on, unaware of the changes."

"I'm not sure it's unaware, according to the news. But yeah, I get your meaning."

Daniel's face drops as he slows down to turn into the square ahead. "Do you? I guess you do, in hiding who you are. I'm doing the same. My parents think I'm depressed and are ready to put me in therapy. Emily keeps saying I need to regain my humanity, but I need to pull away from them."

"Where do they think you are?"

"The only lie I've told them is that I've joined up with the Army. Cross helped Emily out with that. And I have credentials until the next lie happens. It's brilliant, but . . ." His face loses all emotion. The wheel turning in his hands, he looks away. He's always been close with his family. It makes my heart twist for him to leave them in such a way and plan his fake death in order to cut ties.

"But it's a lie."

"Yeah. I don't enjoy doing this to my family. The fact is, I will not age. Did you know that? My aging has slowed exponentially that I will be here when everyone has died." He shakes his head. "It's a lot to come to terms with this rebirth; it's wild and well, I guess it is what it is."

I thoroughly understand Daniel and feel connected. We both are on different paths from where we started last school year—a lifetime ago.

We pull up into a parking space near A Cup of Joe's. It's a small coffee shop that sits next to an old, independent bookshop. It's been here for decades. The couches remind me of a swank old gentlemen's club. Everything is dark wood and forest green, remarkably different from coffee chains. It's unique in its own quirky way.

"So, what are you going to get?" Daniel asks me.

"I think I'm venturing out with a caramel macchiato."

"Oh, that sounds so good. I think I will do the same. Do they have those little scones too?"

I forgot how much he loves blueberry scones. We're teasing each other as we walk into the door and the little bell jingles at the top hinge, wiping away the heavy air of the day.

I hear her voice before I see her. It's Lucy. Daniel's shoulders square and his back straightens. We walk over to the counter and put in our orders for scones and caramel macchiatos. As we turn down the counter, there sits the group: Lucy, Emily, Coral, and Marco.

Emily waves at us. And I look at Daniel, who shrugs, and we walk over to where they are.

"Hey, guys, out for a coffee run?" Coral asks.

"Is it that obvious?" Daniel teases Coral, who immediately smirks.

Lucy shifts in her seat. Her hands touch Marco, who she's sitting next to. He nods at us and leans into Lucy. That's odd. The brief smile she puts on is strained, not authentic. I falter in returning the gesture.

"It's good to see you, Daniel. How are you doing? All good?" Coral asks.

"Yeah, everything is fine. Just thought I'd hang with Willow and grab a drink."

"Obviously," Coral replies. She smirks, and Daniel grins back. Daniel turns his attention to Lucy, who seems to wait with wide eyes before he turns to me and says he's going to check on the order.

Standing there, I'm an outsider. I'm between an invisible wall of tension, one side is Daniel, and the other is Lucy. It's at odds with how it used to be around our friend group.

"So—graduation was crazy," I say to no one directly.

"Yeah, you could say that again," Coral replies. She shrugs nonchalantly, drinking from a mug.

Emily nods, but keeps looking at her cell phone.

"Um. Lucy, your address at graduation was great, by the way."

"Thanks. I was nervous at the beginning but got into the swing."

We flow into simple conversation. Coral and Marco leave for the bathroom when Daniel returns. His stone face, stare and shoulder snub all directed at Marco are surprising.

Lucy says, "Strange huh, how friendships change?"

"What?"

"Ours, there's . . . it's like time has fast forwarded and made things complicated. Sometimes I wish we could go back to prom or before. What about for you, the Senior Camp trip?"

I don't think I would change it. That's when I met Rhydian. I cringe, thinking of Tertium, the blood demon who hunted me in the woods. The first attempt on my life. I nod at Lucy when Daniel stands next to me.

"Yeah, too bad we can't live in the past."

Although his voice quips, it's not accusing or mean.

"Change sometimes can be enlightening. Take

graduation, for example. On the news, the conspiracy theories are all over," Lucy says. "Magick is not something that will be hidden for long."

"Yeah, the storm was crazy, magickal or not."

Lucy's stare makes me squirm. I sit on the edge of a large wingback chair. I look over at Emily, and she shrugs. Her demeanor is at ease, but her eyes wander and assess everything around us.

The girl behind the counter calls mine and Daniel's names for our order. Relieved to be saved from the awkwardness, I turn toward the coffee counter, but I trip on the corner of the claw foot wingback chair. Daniel turns and reaches for me, but it's Marco who is lightning fast. I fall onto my knee and bounce up into Marco's arms, his hands clutching around my waistline.

"Whoa."

Marco tries to spin me away from Daniel as he spills our drinks, but the hot coffee hits my back before going down my leg.

"Get your hands off her!" Daniel shoves his way in between me and Marco.

Lucy is up on her feet. "Oh, good grief, Daniel. Get a grip, it was an accident!"

They argue, and my back is burning. I pull my wet shirt away from my back.

It's Coral who gives me a hand towel. "They're remaking the drinks. Are you okay?"

"Shit, Will. Give me that. I'm sorry." Daniel is behind me with the towel touching my lower back.

"It'll be . . . Oh, damn," I gasp. The burning sensation increases to fire like with the pressure of the towel in Daniel's hand. Did I just see smoke?

"Willow, are you burned?" I hear Marco's tenor voice over Daniel's blockade.

Pulling my shirt away from my skin, it remains hot and wet.

"It's fine," I say to Marco, and repeat myself to Daniel.

I summon my magick into the area of my back and command for my skin to cool. Remembering that I can't use magick, I wince, trying not to show the pain. Marco has an extra hand towel and hands it to me to blot the liquid from my ruined shirt.

"You've done enough," Daniel says to him and grabs the towel. Marco lifts his hands in surrender.

"Whatever, man. What is wrong with you?" Marco turns to Lucy before he walks toward the counter with his mug.

"It was an accident," Lucy says.

"Don't go there, Lucy," Daniel warns.

The tension between Lucy and Daniel surmounts, and the surrounding air thickens. I didn't know they still had so much anger between them.

Putting my hand on Daniel's shoulder. I say as

reassuringly as I can, "I'm fine. It's not a big deal. It's just a shirt."

"See, she said no big deal. Why are you so butthurt over it, anyway?" Lucy lowers her voice. "Not like Willow can't heal herself."

Emily is the only one still seated. She hasn't said two words or even moved from her relaxed state in the chair. It's like she's watching a movie as her head turns from side to side, watching the four of us. It is very unlike Emily to observe from a distance, especially a scene like this. Everyone else who was watching us seem to be back in their own conversations now.

"It's one storm after another," Coral says, when she sits down. "Willow, how are you always in the middle of it?"

"Good question. I don't intend to be."

Lucy's mocking huff pierces my heart a little. It's not as if I seek this stuff . . . or do I?

The barista calls our names again, and Daniel and I go to gather our order with no accidents, ready to leave the awkwardness.

As we leave, I say, "Nice to see you all. Emily, call me."

Emily stays focused on her smartphone. Maybe already texting me?

We close the car doors and set our drinks in the cup holders.

"What was that?" Daniel gestures to the storefront of A Cup of Joe's. "Lucy, Marco? She has changed so much, and I wish I didn't hate her. Hate's a strong word, but I don't like who's she's become."

"You know they aren't together, right?"

Lucy is putting on a show. Marco didn't return any of it, but maybe I misread it? That would be so weird if they were something. I shake my head to rid my mind of the little conspiracy theory. I don't disagree with Daniel, picturing Lucy picking me up to go to school. Us laughing, me making fun of her musical choices. We rarely speak now. Our friendship is changing and has evolved to only acquaintances. She's changed so much I don't recognize her actions anymore. Is it the same for Daniel and Marco? Is that the way of things? The gradual evolution of our friend group upon leaving high school.

"Yeah, I know, but Marco knows better. They both can push my buttons."

Daniel drives us back to my house and we hang out for another hour before he leaves. We avoid discussing our changing friend group.

CHAPTER 4

My head sinks into my pillow, which cradles my weary thoughts like a shield. I stare at the text message from Rhydian and wonder if it was him, or was it Tullen who replied from earlier in the day? I torture myself by scanning through pictures of Rhydian and myself on my phone. The picture Eoin took of us before we left for prom, and the few quick pics during it I took of us. If I had only made him stay, events would have unfolded differently, instead of it becoming the worst prom in history.

Tick-tock.

I shake my head at the image that led to Rhydian leaving. The pressure at my temples is building. I exhale to combat the tension in my neck and shoulders. The thrumming pain in my head, the internal pain, and the squeezing of my chest are all consequences of the broken vow. It didn't just cause Rhydian's suffering; its residual pain is mine too. It pulls and taunts me.

It isn't only a broken heart.

I've had a breakup before, but the physical reaction differs from anything I've experienced before. The only thought I can summon to comfort myself with is that it must serve a purpose. It has to, right? Is it possible we will move beyond what's happened? Will he forgive me? Do I want his forgiveness? His father's intention was to sacrifice me, but he was gambling on the life of his son, too.

I hate that man. The conquest of power poisoned Esmund. He didn't care who he hurt.

Touching a picture of Rhydian on my phone, my finger slides along the smooth surface, aching for a genuine connection, a physical touch, or even the timbre of his voice. I set my phone on my night table and turn on my side and pull my blankets up under my chin.

"Rhydian . . . I'm sorry," I whisper into the dark of my room. Calling to my magick, I try to force myself to sleep within its comfort. My breath is measured and relaxed with each inhale and exhale.

I drift.

The grass is dense and colorful beneath my bare

feet. The moonlight is bright, and I hear the fairies and their music off in the distance. He's here. I see the outline of the blanket ahead. Joy is a liquid elixir that floods through me. The tall reeds are further away from where I stand; I'm near the Lunar Falls. Taking large steps toward the blanket, I turn to see where he is.

"Rhydian? Where are you?" I call out.

"What? I'm right here," he responds.

Behind me, he grabs my waist, pulls me into him, and kisses my neck. His hands on my stomach are warm. I put my hands on his. I turn in his arms and revel in this moment. His face is unmoving, eyes dark, and his forehead touches mine.

The tear that escapes is one I don't wipe away. Blood and dirt cover us both. We are at MacKinnon manor on the grounds. The surrounding has changed.

This is our goodbye. My heartbreak is instantaneous. The kiss I desperately want to remember, but can't. I relive this memory night after night. His hands on my face, the tilt of my chin.

The picture changes, as it has before in my dream. It's the back of him walking away from me; his head hangs from his shoulders. Tullen walking at his hip. I could have called his name, reached for him, but his image waivers in my tear-filled eyes.

The wound is deeper than I want to admit, even

to myself. So many nights my dreams vary, but they always end with Rhydian leaving and me doing nothing.

"Willow. You must stop."

Startled. I turn toward the familiar voice.

It's my uncle Evan. His disheveled appearance familiar except for the plaid pajamas and fluffy unicorn slippers on his feet.

"Goddess, I want to," I reply.

"No, you don't."

He's right, I don't.

The surroundings change, and I'm in a fluffy pink cloud chair across from Evan, who lays back with his arms behind his head in a bright white room.

"Edayri is collapsing into itself. Ol' Esmund was successful in his attempt. Alas, what he didn't know was how unstable he made the entire realm."

"So, you know what is happening?"

"Are you listening at all? Is it your generation, or do I need to do this in a 30-second video, so you'll pay attention?"

"Funny."

I wait, but it's my huff that finally has Evan talking again.

"Edayri is collapsing, Willow. Everyone is being displaced. It's a merger of sorts. Edayrian's are plopping into Terra like the outsiders we are. People here are confused, the Edayrian's dazed—wait, is that a movie?" He looks ridiculous crossing his unicorn feet, then, shrugging his shoulders, he continues. "The point is Edayrian's are refugees now, and they have no option to return, because what's left is dying."

"Edayri is dying?"

Evan's playfulness turns serious.

"Can't you feel it? Beyond your pain of the vow and your broken heart? The countdown, the inevitability of it all? I feel it. I assumed as the embodiment of the Goddess, you would too."

"The countdown? I'm not the embodiment of the Goddess—blessed only, Evan," I say, ignoring his comment about my broken heart. I can't deny it, so why bother? Coward. Is the pulse, the beat, the flutter I feel what he's speaking of? I haven't paid it much attention, thinking it was part of the rift. It's erratic. It is a countdown?

Tick-tock.

Evan's finger swings back and forth to the clock feeling. His eyes wide and waiting.

"Yes, I felt it. I wasn't sure if it had to do with the other—you know, the vow. Him leaving." My uncle's eyes are staring through me, and I glance away from him.

I shake my head trying to push my emotions to the back. "It's stupid. Can I help? I can't sit in this house waiting."

Evan doesn't move. The stare down is creepy, his

eyes moving as if something is playing out in his mind. His half grin plastered on his face.

"Evan?"

He breaks his trance with a quick shake of his head. "Go about a normal day. See your friends, be in town. Take Theon with you wherever you go tomorrow."

"Where were you? Like, just now?"

"Seriously, I'm right in front of you," Evan replies. "Your ability to stay focused is almost as bad as mine."

We both laugh, his booming over mine. Am I losing my mind?

"Can't I help you in Edayri? Surely, I'm more useful there."

"You're useful wherever you are. Have patience, my sweet niece."

Evan smiles, we stand, and I hug him. For a flash, it's like my father hugging me. "Willow, you are anything but a coward. Flex your badass side. You're stronger than you're allowing yourself to be. Don't be what another wants or demands. Be you. That's more than enough," he says.

Light is coming through my curtains, and I wake up. I stretch and the tension in my neck and shoulders are gone. It may be the first night I've slept completely through the night. Duke isn't in my room. My phone shines back to me the time—it's 9:30; I slept in.

Rubbing my eyes, I recall everything so clearly. I remember speaking with Evan. Throwing my covers back, I get ready for the day and to go into town with Theon.

ownstairs, Sabine is opening and closing cabinets in the kitchen. She has a bowl, flour, and milk on the counter.

"What do you need?" I ask.

She turns with her hand on her hip. "Caffeine, for starters. I've got this part. Oh, of course. By chance, how do you operate that intricate-looking machine?" she asks.

A look in her weary eyes says caffeine stat. It's great to know she is like the rest of us and needs a jumpstart in the morning. I open the cabinet next to the cappuccino machine on the counter.

"We call her Fancy, and yes, I steam milk and make coffee and teas. Father used to say I would be the best-trained barista who's never worked in a coffee shop. She's my baby from two Christmases ago."

Sabine laughs, and I smile at the memory of my father presenting Fancy with a big red bow. There are coffee houses that have this exact model. It's extravagant and sturdy. Of course, I love it and use it all the time. I power her up and begin making a cafe latte for us. Sabine is making some kind of pastry that resembles round drop biscuits when both Ax and Theon wander into the kitchen.

"Smells wonderful," Ax says in his deep baritone voice.

"Thank you," Sabine says.

Ax, with wide eyes focused on Fancy, asks, "Where do I find the cups?"

I get a cup that is large but looks like a teacup in his large hands. "As your barista, this morning, would you like lattes or flavors?" I ask.

To my surprise, Ax and Theon both requested mocha lattes, and from the looks on their faces, they surprised each other with the same request. I serve them their requested caffeine.

Ax sits at the table, and I sit at the island and turn toward Theon. I say, "Evan said it's important that we proceed like a normal day, whatever that means. So, how about you come with me for a drive today. See what has happened with this storm?"

Theon nods while drinking his mocha. The storms seem to roll in and out with no warning or pattern. It has stumped meteorologists around the globe. So many conspiracy theories. Most think it's global warming.

"I don't think that's wise. Commander Eoin said to stay put. It's one thing to go out with Daniel, but it's completely another if you're looking for—" Sabine says, bringing a plate piled high of the circle pastry she has made.

"It's not like we're transporting. It's a car ride, like yesterday," I respond.

"It could be helpful to examine what has been affected from yesterday's events. We are isolated in this house; and to what is on the news. Maybe, drive by the school?" Ax adds.

Looking out of the bay window, it looks like it's going to be a beautiful, sunny day. It's quiet as we finish eating. Ax helps Sabine clean the kitchen. The image of a large, blood-demon warrior wiping down and cleaning the table is something I will never unsee. His dark red skin and his horns are intimidating. His six-foot eight-inch frame of muscles, that makes Dwayne Johnson, aka The Rock, look like a skinny kid. Despite all that, here Ax is with a tea towel in hand, talking with Sabine about plans for lunch and dinner.

Theon and I leave and decide we will grab lunch out and take a tour around town. He hides his smaller demon horns by tucking his longer hair back over them in a plait. His style is grungy and relaxed. He has a type of assurance that is comparable to Evan's. I pull out of the drive of the house and turn toward the school.

"Theon, why do you stay around, Evan? Are you good friends?" I ask.

I really know little about Theon, only that Meghan was his sister. Evan's wife. Harkin, the Wiccan King, had Meghan killed because of Evan's defection and rejection of any royal duty on the crown. If I were Theon, I'm not sure I'd want anything to do with Evan or this family.

"We're family. He's my brother," he answers. "Meghan was my sister, but I knew Evan well before they met. Plus, I feel like although Meghan isn't here anymore, that doesn't change who we are to each other."

I nod my head, thinking about how Lucy dated Daniel. Although he's my ex-boyfriend, it doesn't change who she is to me now. She's still one of my best friends, right?

"Why do you ask?"

I turn into the town center. "Well, you risk a lot to support Evan, and even me. The first time I met you, I threw you against a wall to escape." I laugh, remembering when Evan and Theon took me, thinking Rhydian was going to hurt me. My dramatic escape.

He rubs the back of his neck. "That seems so long

ago. I don't hold grudges. Plus, you are important to him, so . . ."

"Do I get to call you uncle too, then?" I laugh, parking the car near the courthouse in the middle of the town square.

He has a kind, calm smile. I think it's the first time I've seen it.

"Absolutely not. My name is fine."

Exiting the car, he pulls on a ball cap and cups the sides of the bill in to shield his eyes. We walk toward the end, past A Cup of Joe's, toward the small Italian eatery. I feel the pulse quickening in my veins and stop walking. Holding my arms at my side, I turn and lean on the storefront nearest to me.

Tick-tock.

"Give me a minute," I say.

"I sense a change in the air too, but it physically affects you?"

Theon watches me with inspecting eyes, nodding toward the bench on the small greenway on the west side of the courthouse. We sit, and I lean forward, prepared for the pain that follows, but it doesn't. It's a small wave and the lights and air shift around us. I spy Lucy with Coral and Coral's stepmother, Vanessa. They are exiting the eatery together. It's strange to see Lucy with Coral's stepmother. Coral is walking ahead of them with her head down, while Lucy and Vanessa are smiling and talking like friends.

I turn and face Theon.

"Did they see us?"

"I don't think so." Theon leans back and is watching them. "They are behind the building, just toward the parking area. She can't see you now—ah, wait. What the—" His face turns serious.

I turn, but Theon is already at a jog, and I follow him, the soft pain subsiding as I move. The pulse, however, remains like a clock in the background of my mind.

The voices are intense and angry, coming from the alleyway between two buildings.

"What the freak are you?" says a deep voice, mocking.

A groan answers and we see something cowered into a lump with two guys standing over it.

"You're one of those that don't belong."

One of them kicks it.

"Stop it!" I yell, scrambling over to the lump.

Theon is squaring off with the men, guiding them away as I get closer to what I expect is a shapeshifter. It's a boy who is half naked, his back cut and bruised. The rift transformed them back into their human form.

Oh, my Goddess, it's Marco!

Barely registering what the guys and Theon are saying to each other. I kneel next to Marco, but before I even touch him, he recoils from me. What did that group do to you? Concealed by the shadows of buildings, I can hardly see him. The unforgiving pavement eats into my covered knee with my full weight on it as I assist Marco. He leans on me.

"I can help," I say, seeking to comfort him. Does he even recognize me?

The yelling increases when I hear Theon.

"You fucking heard wrong."

He inserts himself in front of the jerk, who's outspoken.

"What's it to you?" The taller guy squares himself and pushes Theon.

The smirk on Theon's face is one that says he's ready. Theon is an experienced fighter, and it takes no time for him to hit, kick, and chase them out of the alley.

I call to my magick and feel the hum. My hands light up with the designs I've grown so familiar with. I reach out to touch Marco.

"Don't, Willow, they will see, don't use magick," Marco says through strained breaths.

One of his eyes is swelling. A busted nose. Blood and bruises are all over him. Scraps of a shirt hang on him. He's even lost a shoe. What have those jerks done to him?

"I can't leave you like this. And I dare them to come back." When I say it, my magick flares even brighter. I reach my hand over his shoulder.

"Wait. The rifts, magick isn't reliable, it's—"

"It's reliable with my direct touch, Marco. Trust me?" I ask. My heart squeezes because there is no way I'm leaving him like this.

He nods, and I put my hand on his shoulder. The healing magick I've conjured flows from me to him. His back bends at ease, his neck is no longer straining, and his face is clearing of all cuts and bruises. Gently, he touches my hand. Bloodied gashed knuckles have faded to brown mocha skin that turns soft and taut. I guide my magick as it repairs and knits; the scrapes and the blood disappear. I stand as he moves to sit upright, then stands with me. Healed, he reaches for my hand and his lips lift to the corner of one side.

"Thank you. And we should probably go somewhere else," Marco says, worry creasing his forehead and his eyes looking behind me.

Theon is walking toward us with a hoodie and Marco's missing shoe.

Marco puts on the hoodie and slips on his shoe. I look back at the town square. "Do you want to go to the diner?"

He leads the way. Theon and I follow him in silence. The door chimes to alert the waitress, and she gestures to the booth along the window.

After she takes our order and walks away, I ask, "Marco, what happened? Who was that?"

"It wasn't those hunters, just some assholes. I had a shifting phase that happens because of the rift, and I tried to get into the alleyway unnoticed, but those guys saw me."

"Hunters? Wait, what?"

"I'm not sure of their true name, but they are organized and seeking those with magick. Word is spreading about them. They are hurting and killing."

I can't believe it, hunters. Or even in this case that someone saw something unexpected, and their initial thought would be to harm someone?

They should try it with me.

My magick is at the ready in the background. I feel the steady hum rise on the surface of my skin. I take a deep inhale of air to calm myself. The shimmer and glow fades, but it's there. I'm concealing my magick from everyone in the diner, including Theon and Marco.

"I can't believe they even approached you," I say.

He falls back in his seat and rolls his eyes. "Willow, look at me. Just my skin color already has me at a disadvantage for prejudice. If I add shifting to it— I'll be enemy number one. I'd rather fade into the background right now." Marco's eyes wander around us, before he continues as a group of girls walk into the diner, "This is your standard, good ol' hate crime."

"It's happening everywhere, isn't it?" Theon asks.

I stir my soda with my straw. Gah, I hate the way some people lash out at differences.

"Yeah, can you imagine if you couldn't glamour to be us even? You better hide or find a new home elsewhere, 'cause you're going to be at the top of that list. I guess I'm lucky that at least I have my human form, which is my stable side." Marco pauses. "My little brother, on the other hand, he has trouble not being stable. It's the case for most youth right now."

The waitress brings us our lunch orders.

"I'm so sorry, Marco."

"It's my fault for leaving the house, I suppose. My folks left for my aunt's farm in Idaho with my younger brother. I'm supposed to tie up loose ends here and meet them there. But thankfully, mail is all forwarded now, and I should be able to leave in the next day or so." He shrugs it off and takes a big bite of his apple pie. I'm saddened to think the hate for his skin color is not unexpected for him, regardless of the magickal rifts.

I'm so naïve.

"Marco, this is going to sound stupid, but how are you getting to Idaho?" I ask.

"Driving, why?"

"Well, as you mentioned with the rifts and shifting, maybe it isn't wise to drive."

He turns and opens his mouth before he says, "Ah, I don't—"

"Hear me out. How about you stay at my house. You can keep an eye on your house, and I have plenty of room. Shifting there is no problem, because, well, my closest neighbor is nearly a mile away in a private estate."

Theon makes this face that I can't quite read. He squints his eyes and almost smirks.

"I don't want to put you out or anything," Marco says.

"Seriously, you've seen the mausoleum of my home. We have plenty of room. You can have any of the remaining bedrooms."

Marco looks from me to Theon. "That's really cool of you. Are you sure? 'Cause, hell, I'm not sure I can keep it together in here, to be honest. Everything is unpredictable right now."

It's late afternoon when we drive back to the house. Marco is going to his house first to gather a few things before he comes over to my house.

The rift noise seems to have stopped for a moment. I expect that Sabine and Ax will have a ton of questions, so Theon and I decide we will call them in the car and explain instead of having them bombard us right at the door.

"Willow, you need to be careful out in the open, because you attract magick," Theon says.

"I can't sit on my hands, Theon. You saw what happened to Marco."

His face is unreadable.

"I'm saying we can't roam the streets looking. We need a coordinated plan. I wholeheartedly agree, what happened isn't right."

"Well, what does a coordinated plan look like? Do you think Evan expected we'd find Marco? And he knew we'd be able to help him?"

His grumble is preceded by, "No telling with Evan, but most likely."

If that is true, thank Goddess.

CHAPTER 6

Outside, everything from the front window of the sitting room is green and lush, full of life. I watch as Emily's car pulls in at the front of the house. Marco and I are at the door when we see Daniel opening the car door. I smile and wave at the sight of both of them, but Marco's shoulders square off.

"What's up with you and Daniel?" I ask in a quiet voice.

"He's different. The ego won't fit in your foyer right now."

His lips curve into a mocking smile as Daniel walks up the stairs.

We all walk into the house, and I barely register the large duffle bag that Daniel swings off his back onto the floor.

"What's this? Do you need somewhere to stay?"

Marco clinches his jaw at my question.

Daniel looks from Emily to me before Emily speaks up.

"Yeah. Daniel needs a better permanent stop, and I thought since you had all this room, it would be okay?"

She lifts her hands in a slight gesture, and her eyes open wide, awaiting my response. As if I would say no. This must be the favor she didn't elaborate on when I called her about what happened to Marco.

"Of course, absolutely. It won't be a problem. You can take the guest room across from mine. Cross and Quinn are here too."

I watch Emily as she shifts her weight at the mention of Cross's name.

"Maybe this isn't a good idea," Daniel replies.

"Well, it's up to you. I'm okay either way."

"Marco, what say you?" Daniel asks.

Marco's shoulders relax. "Yeah, man, it's fine. But I'm not taking any more crap. I've got my own shit right now with this ongoing magickal chaos. Feel me?"

Emily and I watch the two of them like a tennis match.

"Deal. It's off the table then."

"Good, because for the last time, it never should have been on the table."

Men, direct and to the point; once something airs,

then it's dealt with. I wonder if Emily, Lucy, and I will ever be like we were before. I miss our trio.

Daniel's half-grin is easy, and he leans in and kisses me on the cheek. Then he hugs Marco in a macho half-hug kind of way.

"Man, I'm glad you're okay," Daniel says to Marco.

Marco laughs and says, "Yeah, me too, thanks to Willow and Theon."

Daniel picks up his duffle, and they make their way to the stairs.

Emily points toward the kitchen. "I'd die for your famous latte."

In the kitchen, I start up the cappuccino machine and ask, "What was that with Daniel and Marco, anyway? Where does Daniel's family think he's gone to?"

"Just a misunderstanding with Lucy. She's been starting a little trouble with Daniel."

That doesn't sound like Lucy at all. She always avoided crazy antics, unlike Emily. For her to be playing games with Daniel, someone she loves is off from her personality.

"Daniel's family thinks he's off to Army boot camp. Little do they know it's an immortal military type of boot camp. Plus, my place is just as nutty with me moving out and finding other living arrangements away from the foster parents."

"Emily, they aren't foster parents," I reply.

Although Emily's mannerism says carefree, it's a facade. Her hair is dull, and her skin is pale. "But they aren't my real parents, either. I need to break the magickal ties as quickly as possible to keep them out of all this. Hell, it's awkward as it is because the rifts are playing with magick all over the place. I almost got hit with a bat during one attempt because they thought I was robbing the place."

She pretends she doesn't care, but I know she has loved living with her parents and Brody, her big brother, for the last several years. She magicked them with a spell so that they think they've always known her as their daughter. I wonder how she will break the magickal tie. Will they remember her at all? I know Emily. She has a hard exterior, but inside she is mourning the loss of yet another family. I hug her before I hand her the latte. We have a lot in common.

Cross sweeps in, turning on his foot, and laughing with Duke on his heels in some kind of chase. "Easy, yes, I'll get you a treat—"

"Hey," Emily says and smiles weakly at him.

He nods up but says nothing back. Instead, he returns his attention to Duke and, before grabbing Duke's treat, he turns. "Willow, Evan is coming by shortly."

Cross turns to leave, but stops when I say, "Hey, we have a new resident."

Cross's jaw sets.

"Daniel is going to be here for a while," I say.

I barley register the audible sigh from Emily.

He nods and walks out of the kitchen with Duke on his heels. Although eager to hear from Evan and get the details on what's going on, I turn my attention to Emily, who is staring out the window. Her downcast eyes and the sniffle of her nose say it all.

"Em, what's going on with you and Cross? Is there something I can do?" I ask.

Her face falls. What little light there was but a moment ago in her face it's vanished. No pretense at all. She looks how I feel. "No, there is nothing to be done. It's gotten complicated, but it'll work out . . . or not," she replies.

"You know I'm a superb listener. I totally get complicated. Have you seen my life? Oh right, you've witnessed most of it." We both laugh as a tear escapes her eye. "When you're ready, know I'm here." Before I can say anymore, I'm being hugged, and I gently return it. I could have sworn I heard her say, I wish I could.

Evan slides into the entryway of the kitchen dramatically with no shoes, only socks.

"I've always wanted to do that."

I laugh as he balances himself.

"Thank Goddess. He's not in his underwear," Emily laughs.

"What?"

I'm shaken to the core. I do not need to see my uncle in his underwear. Thankfully, Evan is fully dressed in jeans and a collared shirt that is open with a white tee-shirt. Definitely an improvement from pajamas and unicorn slippers.

"Eighties movie." Em shakes her head at me.

Evan smiles and points at Emily. "Yes, but they don't have this." He holds a hand up, and a light orb forms. I'm excited to see the fully formed magick in his hand is solid and nothing crazy is happening.

"Damn it!" Cross yells from the office before we hear a loud crash.

We all get to Cross in my father's office quickly. He is soaking wet as if he was in a dunk tank. Duke is shaking his body, and water is going everywhere.

"What happened?"

"I was communicating with Tullen before we got separated, and then the magick broke and literally washed away." He shakes his enormous arms, and the water falls to the floor in a puddle. "Any chance that yer magick or Evan's is a little more reliable that ya can dry me off quickly without setting me on fire?"

"Because that has happened?" I ask as I roll my eyes, shaking my head, knowing that most likely it has.

Before Evan can say something strange, I step in front of Cross and place my hands on his shoulder and call to my magick and command the air to dry him and clear the water from the room. It comes up like cool steam before it disappears in front of our eyes.

"Showoff." Evan smiles and winks.

"I'm glad it worked. Feels good to use it in any capacity."

Evan laughs, but Cross's lips are in a thin line. I follow his eyes to Emily.

"Still here?" Cross snaps more than asks. The tension in the air is thick. Emily squares her shoulders.

"Really? Is this your house or Willow's?" Emily bites back. She turns to Evan and me. "There is another reason I'm here, Willow, besides the great latte and Daniel. I need to talk with you, and it works out that Evan's here."

"I do know the importance of timing, like no other," Evan replies, then nods his head toward the sitting arrangement in front of the window. Daniel and Marco come into the office. Cross extends his fist, and Marco pounds it like they are old pals.

What have I missed in the last twenty-four hours?

"Let's let them chat, fellas." Cross ushers them out the door. But not be before Daniel eyes us warily.

Emily sits down in front of Evan.

"It feels like it was before, in the Norse realm. I'm not sure how to describe it, but this is going to be permanent, Willow. The chaos and displacement. Maybe even the control of magick? I'm not sure."

"This is our Ragnarök," Evan says, not asking. Emily nods, her eyes cast down before she shrugs her shoulders.

"Could it be the same?" I ask. As soon as I say it, I recall how Emily told me about how her realm collapsed.

"It's what you call the Convergence—semantics," Emily replies.

"Toma-toe, Tam-ah-to. Still the same gross veggie," Evan says. His facial features pinch tight, despite the off-handed comment.

Quinn enters from the hidden library where my father's coven space is. His face has ash streaks at the temples and his fingertips. "Oh, hello." He sits next to me on the small couch. "What's up?"

"Did you find anything helpful?" I ask Quinn.

"I believe we've found a way to transport reliably. The legion council has found patterns in the rift of Convergence, an open timing that is uninhibited." I must have looked like a deer in headlights because Quinn shakes his head as if to clear his mind. "Basically, transporting safely with a magickal pass that overwrites the rifts as they do now. They are working out the kinks."

"That is good news," Em says to Quinn.

"It is and isn't," Evan says, but no one gives him notice except me. Although he's full of riddles, Evan's insight and power are essential. He continues, "tell us about the Norse realm. How did you come to Edayri? What led you there?"

"When we found Edayri, a series of events set off Ragnarök: battles, the death of Odin, elemental disasters. Willow, this feels the same, and I'm worried that the only realm to inhabit is here, in Terra."

"But that's okay, right?"

No one is looking at me. They all seem to study the room. I feel stupid staring at Evan. Yes, I'm that naïve.

Quinn turns to me. "Willow, the collapse of any realm, especially one of magick, is not okay. Who knows what effect it will have here, on Terra, which is quite populated. Also, our population is full of different species that rarely pass as humans. You have already seen what happens. Look at Marco."

Emily stands and thrusts her hands through her hair. "Exactly. Edayri was built by gods and is fueled by magick itself. Do you think all creatures would be welcomed here? Willow, it's not safe for anyone with any abilities. If you wanted magick to be hidden for you here—it's just not . . ." The silence drags before Emily speaks again, but she looks directly at Evan. "There are magick hunters here on Terra. That's what happened to Marco," Emily says, and all eyes focus on her.

Evan silently walks to the tall window and looks

out as if searching for something. "Because we've seen it before, haven't we, Quinn?"

Emily is the first to respond. "We noticed that those with higher powers were targets that attract attention. Several of my family members were hunted and killed here just for blatant displays of power. They did not welcome us in Edayri, but it was safer than here." Her eyes are wary and distant. Emily focuses on her hands and intertwines her fingers in a pattern, back and forth. "The fact Willow, you have Goddess powers, and Evan, you have Horned God powers. What Marco experienced? It's not any different. There will be more hunters. It's a lot like my past. Your combined power and nearness to each other is going to be a calling of magick."

"A calling of magick?" I ask.

"Yes. Calling like to like, kindred spirits will gather."

Evan laughs as if he just told himself a private joke.

"What?" Cross's voice booms in the room when he enters. "Ya should have said something before now! What is wrong with you?"

Quinn stands and puts his hand on Cross's shoulder.

"So, what do we do?" I ask.

I'm energized at the thought of a task. It's got to be better than staying out of the way as others handle what's going on in Edayri. I'm not letting anyone hurt anyone with magick because they are different.

Emily answers, "You need to be in a different place than Evan. You can't be together for any length of time—"

"Do you know who these hunters are?" Cross is in front of Emily, his shoulders tense, and his face is stone. "Is Willow safe here?"

Shit. Cross is hurdling over the line and being too aggressive, almost accusing her of something. Emily doesn't retreat from him. She stands firm and looks like she may hit him with lightning if he isn't careful.

"There are magickal wards on this house. But all of us being here right now is a risk? Is that what you're saying? That it is because of the individual powers we possess?" I ask.

Emily nods in confirmation of my question. Evan is looking at everyone. He turns before he speaks. "You'll be safe here. I'm needed elsewhere, somewhere over the rainbow." His head tilts like he is listening to someone no one else can hear. He nods, as if satisfied with himself.

The magick shows on my skin and pulses with liquid-like light patterns. I'm sure the crown is floating above my head. I'm sick of being sidelined. What, am I supposed to sit here on my hands? Eoin and the Guardians have tasks for helping those who are displaced. All while I'm sitting on my ass. This is such utter bullshit, especially if there are hunters here in Terra.

"Why?" I ask no one.

Evan answers me after a pause. "Oh, if I had a dime, for every time that simple question has been asked."

Cross claps him on his back and says, "What, you'd have a dollar and fifty cents?" The tension cuts with chuckles and laughter.

Emily leans into me. "I've got to get back. Anyway, Willow, be careful and be mindful of what's happening."

I walk Emily to the front door and hug her good-bye. When the front door shuts, a loud sound echoes from the heavy door. The jolting sound vibrates from my hand up my arm. I stand alone in the house's foyer.

PART II

*An inward reflection and surrender of the full moon, weighs
on decisions and acceptance.*

-The Horned God

CHAPTER 7

It's been a couple of days since Daniel came to stay at my house. Sabine is making fresh pasta for dinner. I'm tucked away in the private coven room behind the bookcase in my father's office.

I'm learning more about my family in the Book of Shadows. Who, unfortunately, isn't answering my questions directly. I keep reading it repeatedly. The eight-ball type answers given are not direct answers.

Typical.

Tick-tock.

I hate the radio silence from the outside world and not fully knowing what is happening in Edayri. It was only yesterday the news reported on television: the storms globally are part of the environmental changes. The unfortunate part is it's also bringing up discussions about refugees and the increase in other strange phenomenon. I cringe at a spokesperson who said that we need to police our community and alert the authorities of suspicious, otherworldly behavior. I can imagine the looks on people's faces when they come across a demon or someone who is a shifter, mid-reveal or transformation as a result of the rift. A Wiccan is easy to hide, unless they transport in front of a crowd.

Knock. Knock.

"Hello?" I ask, secretly hoping I don't see Sabine's bright red hair coming around the corner.

Instead, the tall shadow reveals my uncle, Evan, who enters the coven room.

"Evan! I'm surprised to see you. What are you doing here? Does—"

He shakes his head and smiles. I greet him with a hug and can't help the small tear that escapes my eye. The rush of movement ignites a throbbing pain in my head.

He touches my temple and says, "Worry not."

An immediate liquid feeling of relief floods my mind. The beat that is always thrumming in my head is quickly a quiet whisper. He's used magick on me to ease my pain. That makes me want to cry more, but in relief, because popping medicine has done nothing. Drinking gallons of water per Sabine's constant orders has done nothing but make me pee every hour. I pull back from him while he holds my shoulders and studies my face.

"What's wrong?" I ask. Trying to contain the quiver in my voice.

"Not unless you call this Convergence wrong? But then again, what's wrong is putting things right, but either way it's painful; change always is."

Evan and his riddles. His wandering mind is something I now cherish.

"Not what I meant. You're here. I thought that transporting and magick were only to be used in dire need, or for the Guardians and Council."

I touch my temple where he used magick to ease my constant pain.

He shrugs.

"We're figuring it out. Come, I'm not alone and have the 411."

He turns and walks through the short, concealed hallway, the lanterns extinguishing as we leave. My heartbeat is present in my ears, with a pulling sensation at my ribs. I close the open bookcase door and find Abigail, Rhydian's sister.

"Willow!" Abigail launches herself at me and hugs me tight, and I reciprocate.

Sabine enters, wiping her hands on an apron.

"Abby, I'm happy to see you."

It isn't completely true. I do like Abby but seeing her only reminds me that Rhydian is absent. I think of the broken blood vow, which causes the constant pain that Evan just relieved me of.

"What report do you bring?" Sabine asks. She sets down a platter as if this is some grand social visit and she expected company.

Abigail and Evan look at each other. She exhales before explaining, "MacKinnon Manor is sinking into the land because Edayri is breaking apart with the collapse. Your house staff are working to save what they can in terms of cherished house items. They've requested your assistance in the move to Terra."

Abby continues, "The Royal Guardian's will protect the Queen at this residence for the foreseeable future, per the Commander's orders. However, I'm here to retrieve you."

"I can help you, Sabine." The opportunity to leave the house and see Edayri is a lure.

Evan is the first to respond. "No, Willow, you're to stay here. There is more need for you here."

Before I can respond, Sabine and Abby are repeating Evan.

"What? Why should I stay here? I'm sure I can do more in Edayri," I almost yell, like a child.

Sabine places her hand on my shoulder.

"We don't know what they are facing in the collapse of Edayri and that is dangerous, Willow. The fact that it isn't immediate and seems in stages . . . we have to be careful. Who knows when this could change? We must follow Eoin's instructions," Sabine says. The voice of reason. But then again, she won't be stuck in Chepstow under guard.

"But MacKinnon Manor . . . is really sinking?"

Evan is dramatic when he crosses over toward the windows. "Like a yellow submarine."

"When do we leave?" Sabine asks Abby.

"In just under an hour." Abby looks at her watch. "Only pack necessary items, if any."

Sabine nods. "Okay. We have enough time to eat. How about a quick bite?"

How can they eat and act as if this is a normal day? I smile awkwardly, watching Sabine and Evan leave with his lazy steps in a delay. Leaving me alone with Abigail. My stomach knots, knowing she will ask about her brother.

"Have you heard from Tullen and Rhydian?" She moves closer to me on the couch.

I adjust by turning my knee on the couch to put distance between us. I want to say yes, I've heard from them. But the disappointing part is I haven't since graduation, when the Convergence started, and now I'll have to admit that to her. It makes it more real verses continuing to be ghosted. "No, I haven't." Pursing my lips, I try to look anywhere except at her large pitying eyes that are similar in color to Rhydian's.

"Have you?" I ask, my voice feeling small.

"Only briefly."

Why does my chest feel heavy? The squeeze of air that escapes my lungs as if I'm being hit without expecting it. Of course, he would reach out to her. She's, his sister. What am I in his world? Am I his girlfriend anymore? The crack widens; the fissure that seems impossible to close. I'd rather have the headache Evan magicked away.

"I'm sure he'll reach out soon to you. He's looking for our mother and he's torn and struggling too, Willow."

He's looking for his mother. My heart aches and I should be supportive, but all I can think about is my selfish ass.

"I feel inconsequential—Abby, the blood vow is broken. It's like something is missing from me and I can't repair it without—Hell, I don't know if it can be fixed. I've tried a few things but—"

Evan's voice is there before I see him. He must have stayed nearby. He says, "An ache of a broken blood vow is not partnerless. It takes two to tango."

"What?"

Abby turns in shock, as if what I said was the ramblings of a broken-hearted babbling girl. Aren't I though?

Duke follows Evan into the living room, his tail wagging in greeting. Evan pets his head when he sits in a chair across from us.

"Willow, tell me I'm wrong?" he asks me.

"It's true but, I've got used to it. I can sleep fitfully at night. There is something else like a—"

"Clock," he fills in. "Since graduation when it began?" Evan is speaking about the Convergence as if it's different from the broke blood vow pain.

"Oh, my Goddess, Willow, if he knew—" Abby says.

Right if Rhydian knew? I tighten my jaw because I want to yell at her. If he knew what? That the broken vow causes me pain? That would bring him back, but nothing else? His duty and loyalty over his personal feelings?

I take a quick breath to steady myself. I don't want to put my frustrations on Abby.

"Doesn't matter, he's not reaching out and talking to me," I say.

Abby shakes her head, as if clearing off too many thoughts. "I just don't understand, the blood vow. Rhydian took the vow seriously. If he knew he was causing you direct pain, he would be beside himself."

"I wish that he never gave me that damn blood vow. I've doubted so much, and I'll never know what was real or just influenced by the vow. Now it's all gone except for this hollowing ache and pain."

"He didn't give you the blood vow directly. He gave it to Aiden," Evan says as Duke rolls on his back for the scratches to continue on his tummy by Evan.

He's right! I didn't accept the blood vow directly. My father did this on my behalf.

"Oh!" I suck in my breath so fast I cough. "You're right!" Why didn't I figure this out?

Abby looks from Evan to me and asks, "You didn't accept the blood vow directly?"

She is smiling, and I can't help but laugh mockingly.

"No, I didn't. I didn't even know what it was. But —what does this mean? Can it be reversed? My father is no longer—"

The vow didn't die with him. Remembering my father, my hero, my magick hums to life on my skin. My father asked me to trust Rhydian.

I think about Rhydian and see his face clearer than I have in my mind for the last week. His stormy ocean eyes when he's troubled or serious versus the clear blue in happiness. His dimpled cheeks that only show in a full smile. My heart pulls in my chest and my ribs constrict. The familiar hurt of the broken blood vow.

I didn't want this. Maybe I can reverse it or better yet, absolve it? I have royal powers, why not?

Evan interrupts my thoughts. "Rhydian will not agree to any reversal or spell. He feels responsible and likes the pain, the reminder."

Did Evan read my mind? Rhydian likes the pain. Typical. He would punish himself.

"I will talk to him and—" Abby says.

I interrupt, "No, I need to talk to him."

More like he needs to talk to me. I forced his betrayal by helping him hurt me, which broke the tenants of the vow. "Right now, the connection is our pain. He needs to talk to me, Abby. You can't solve this for him or for me."

Will there be us? The pain in my ribs makes it hard to breathe. I feel heavy but stand against the emotion that's holding me in place. I walk out of the living room and go to my room with Duke on my heels. His head nudges my hand where I lay on my bed. I hug him, petting and rubbing his sweet face, and cry silently.

◈

I overhear Quinn ask where Evan and Theon are when I enter the living room.

"They are discussing something in the kitchen. Their time for transporting is coming up in the next several minutes."

Now transporting occurs only by specific points of departure and entry. I'm not really sure how they figure this out, along with the beating pulse like thumps of the rifts and the changes in the air. It's not a consistent thing. And it's not necessarily something that is regulated, but Evan says it has a pattern.

Cross and I follow Quinn into the kitchen.

Theon claps Cross on the back. "How goes it?" Theon asks. I never realized they knew each other, but it makes sense.

"Good enough."

Evan is in front of me. His eyes are piercing.

"Are you okay, Evan?" I get a brief hug before he lets me go. "Why do I feel you're not telling me something?"

He winks, then pats my head like a child.

"Seriously," I push at him. "What is going on besides the fact that I feel like I won't see you again? I don't like being kept in the dark."

"Don't fear the dark—"

"I don't! You're hiding something important from me. I'm not a child!"

He says nothing. It feels like a confirmation before he says, "It's unclear how events will play out, so I'd rather not play at something that I could influence wrongly. That's something Doc Brown warned Marty about in that movie. Its good advice."

What can I say to that? This scrambled view of the future Evan sees is because of magick I cast when we were fighting each other. Although often confusing, he now considers it a gift, and I'm not sure he's wrong. I'm connected to him not only by family but by a destiny I'm still unclear about. It has to do with

Goddess and the Horned God. It's a family legacy for the ages, or so Sabine and Tullen have told me.

Quinn comes over and says, "I think it's time for you and Theon to transport. You have a five-minute window in which to transport to the Hallowed Hall. Eoin will meet you. Ax will be there, Theon, and he will provide you with details for lodging within the Guardian grounds. Abigail and Sabine, it's the same entry point."

Evan smiles and moves to the foyer of the house. Cross opens the front door. "Actually, it's better if you are outside, for transporting."

Quinn gives me a look, and I follow him outside to the front yard. The advantage of living on private estate grounds is that my neighbors are far enough away that they won't see or notice anything.

Evan and Theon stand together, and Theon touches Evan's shoulder. They look like old pals and friends. The wind swirls around them and I notice a flock of birds coming overhead as Evan and Theon disappear. A bird lands in the yard. Sabine gives me a quick hug before she and Abigail do the same. They disappear in an instant.

The bird on the ground is squawking loudly. Duke launches himself from the porch and the bird takes flight just in time.

CHAPTER 8

It's late afternoon. I'm on the couch with one foot lazily rubbing Duke's side when Cross and Quinn find us.

"Hey, Willow. We need to talk with you," Quinn says, sitting across from me.

Cross enters a code on his Guardian wrist cuff, and a light bounces around the room.

"To ensure we're having a private conversation."

"About the patrols? You know what happened when Theon and I found Marco. Is it more hate crimes?"

Quinn only nods. Cross's jaw juts out.

"Listen, don't you dare shield me like I'm a dainty flower. Tell me what is going on! I've been through hell this past year, so it's not like I can't take it. Plus, I should fucking know." I steady my voice as much as I can.

Quinn looks at me straight in the eyes. "No one, and I mean, no one, knows better than we do what you've been through in the last year. We know you are more than capable. As our Queen, we are here as your royal Guardians to report. That being said, it's for your ears only."

I sit a little straighter, and Cross grabs my attention when he huffs, "Will, I'll give it to ya straight. It's a shit show. Sometimes we patrol and find corpses. Other times, we transport the lost to where we have the refugee camps and try to reunite families. Other times, it's nothing but fear. It varies day to day."

"I'm not useless." I flex my hand, and my magick dances over my skin with a white flame as I move it finger to finger before clutching it in my hand. "I don't understand why the legion council, and everyone wants me to stay here. I could be helping."

"Magick doesn't solve everything. Willow, these hunters follow the path of magick. If you use your magick, you could do more damage than you intend to. Innocents could get caught in the middle. You're a magick beacon with your power."

Quinn's right, and I wouldn't say I like it.

"So, pretend it's a normal day?"

"Well, when have you had a normal day?" Cross laughs.

True. Every time I leave this house, something happens: graduation, A Cup of Joe's, and Marco?

"Having the two of you as my babysitters is not normal, Quinn."

Cross covers his heart as if he's hurt. "Right, so we pull together a schedule. Training, study, the whole thing. I'm not the babysitting type. I'm a Royal Guardian and, hopefully, a friend. So, let's get it straight in yer head."

He's right. Sitting on my ass isn't helping me, anyway. I might as well train and prepare, because I'm not useless and can't play that part. I need to be ready for anything.

"Okay," I say in agreement.

"So, here's the deal. We don't want Daniel and Marco involved in Guardian business and updates that we give to you." My inhale stops Quinn, but only for a moment. "You may trust them, and we get it; they are great. However, now everything is sensitive and confidential information per Commander orders."

I shrug. "All right, then we meet every day. This is just a precaution, right?"

They both nod.

"So, it's okay for my friends to come over here then?" I ask.

"Certainly, that's something we can contain better here at the house."

"Sure. Who's coming over?" Quinn asks.

"Emily," I reply.

Cross's exhale is something I don't press since he won't look me in the eye. I'm not sure what's occurred between him and Emily, but I will ask her tomorrow.

"Is that a problem?"

"Nah. Not a problem. This house is enormous enough that I won't be seen," Cross says before tapping his wrist cuff, and he turns out of the room.

I look at Quinn for an explanation. He shrugs before he says, "Cross isn't keeping secrets, but he's hurt. He won't admit that. It comes out as hostility and anger, but he'll simmer down."

I want to press for more information, but who am I to get involved? My relationship status is non-communicative at this point. Maybe he reads it on my face.

"She said she didn't have time for him, and they've been fighting about Lucy. Emily feels she has an obligation to Lucy, her niece, and Cross feels that Lucy uses Emily. It's been radio silent for about a week, so the wound is oozing."

"Why would he think Lucy is using Emily?" I ask.

Quinn is hesitating.

"You will not hurt my feelings. Tell me."

"All right." He steals a glance toward the open doorway. "We don't trust her. She seems to have conflicting motives about magick and who she is. According to Marco, she guilts Emily all the time. She also manipulates Daniel, and they still speak a lot, but they are constantly arguing."

That is so strange. Daniel acted like they had nothing in common anymore and rarely speak. She was acting weird at A Cup of Joe's, almost taunting Daniel with Marco sitting next to her as if they were on a date. Daniel was upset with Marco, but clearly Marco wasn't giving Lucy the same attention.

"It's odd. Should I talk to Daniel about it?"

"No. Let's keep this as a confidential discussion. We have watchers out on the situation. They are magickal, and there is concern right now for the safety of all misplaced Edayrians. Let them go about their business. We honestly don't have the manpower, anyway."

"Okay, but I can't act like I know nothing."

"Yes, you can. You don't want to bring any attention to this. Let it all play out."

I nod in agreement, but not sure I can do that. Daniel is staying here. What if someone is in danger? A shiver climbs down my spine and I stand up, taking a deep breath. Duke is at my heels.

Tick-tock.

CHAPTER 9

The last few days passed quickly because of the routine I agreed to with Cross. Every morning I train with Cross in our basement gym. I like physical training because I can't think about anything but the present, what is in front of me. My arms and legs are stronger. I'm getting better, faster, and more daring where it pays off.

Cross, Quinn, Marco, and Daniel are my norm. We all eat together and chill in front of the television together. Marco and Daniel seem to have worked out their tension and are back to being their typical selves. The days seem to go by, until the stillness of the dark in my room, when I think about Rhydian. I don't stay in my room much anymore. I wander around this massive house with Duke at my heels.

Tap, tap, and pow.

I hit Cross's padded hands and dodge his overhead swings, one and two.

"Combo," Cross says.

I kick and hit Cross's padded body. I smile when he uses his back foot to anchor himself. Daniel pops up and taps me out when he lunges away from Cross, who takes the offense.

"Nice, Danny," Cross says, and he smiles.

I stretch my calves sitting next to Quinn.

"You're quite good at fighting, Willow." He hands me a water bottle.

"Thanks, I am improving for sure."

I watch Cross direct Daniel. "Cross is a talented trainer. I'm careful not to say that too loud." I chuckle.

"Oh, trust me, he knows it. That's okay"—Quinn raises his voice— "he still can't play Black Ops for shit against me!"

Wrinkles form on Cross's forehead, his lips a thin line. He focuses on Daniel, who is attacking him with various punching combos and a roundhouse kick. Daniel has gotten great at fighting.

I nudge Quinn. "Hey, are you taking another shift tonight?"

Quinn and Cross have been taking various Guardian shifts for patrols, helping with refugees nearby. My goal is to go with them. Daniel and Marco are eager to help, too. They have urged me to talk to

Quinn. We all have cabin fever and need help. I know I need a function besides being guarded behind glass windows.

"Most likely. The work is increasing, and we don't have as many Guardians covering the whole of the Edayrian population."

"So, I have an idea. How about me, Daniel, and Marco accompany you."

Quinn shakes his head. "The commander gave strict instructions because it's too volatile. Plus, the enchantments put on this property will warn everyone and anyone at the Hallowed Hall."

"Oh, how I love being under lock and key like this." I slink back onto the concrete wall and slide to where I can place my arms on my knees straight out. "I want to see what you're seeing. I've been practicing, and I can control my magick through direct touch. It could be useful. Besides, you guys have a harder time controlling magick."

"It won't be like this forever."

"Don't put me on some pedestal like I'm breakable. I haven't broken yet, despite everything."

Quinn nods with confirmation.

That's an unsettling notion, forever a future. What is mine? Deferrals for college? I'm not even sure if that is what I want to do anymore. Being left out of the loop with Edayri, I'm just a figurehead to be protected. I am the Wiccan Queen and have powers that most only dream of, but they don't want me involved. I am a spectator, and it sucks.

Duke barks, and I startle when I hear him.

Bam.

I turn to see another bird hit the small window high on the basement wall. Then a third, almost as if it was flying into the house, but didn't notice it. I run out to the front yard, and there are about twenty birds. I squat down to one and call to my familiar hum.

Marco, in his tiger form, is running from the back of the yard.

"No! Don't heal it!" Quinn yells behind Cross.

"Why? It shouldn't harm them if I touch them—"

"That's not the point." Cross frowns and looks around the yard and runs off to the left, yelling, "Marco, shift back if you can or get in the house!"

Daniel moves to the side as Marco runs through the back door.

I point at the birds. "This is cruel. What is this?"

Quinn shakes his head. "We aren't sure, but every time I go to investigate a magickal death, there are small dead animals like this around. Not everyone has controllable magick like you do, since the rifts, and we expect these animals are used to identify those who have magick. Could Marco have triggered it? The wards around the house don't go too far."

Cross comes from the right, having run around

the house, and his hands are up, and there is a force barely visible to my own eyes that is shrouding the house in a protective spell.

Quinn flexes his hands, and the Guardian wrist band expands his armor over his lean body. Cross does the same. They pick up the dead birds and place them in a magicked bag of some sort that disposes of the poor little birds.

Is this an omen of things to come, more death? I'm not ready for more death, but then again, is anyone?

In the house, I find Daniel. Marco is pacing in his tiger form in the sitting room.

"Marco isn't able to shift back at the moment, so we're just waiting it out," Daniel says.

"Cross and Quinn are cleaning up the yard. The birds are cursed or something, so when Marco shifted it may have alerted them here?" Shrugging at Marco when his big bulky body stops at my words mid-stride. "It's insane, right?"

"Insane? Kind of brilliant."

My head snaps at Daniel. Did he say that it was brilliant?

"I mean . . . if you want to ferret out something inconspicuously, this is an interesting way to do it."

"I guess, but the poor birds are dead, Daniel. They are dead."

Daniel shrugs, monitoring Marco. I don't like how

dismissive he is to the birds. I'm not used to his indifferent response.

"Daniel?"

"Yeah?"

"Are you okay? I know it's a lot to be cooped up in this house. I asked Quinn about joining him and Cross tonight."

His eyes light up. "He said yes?"

"Not yet." I smile.

"You can be convincing when you put your mind to it, Willow."

What an odd thing to say. I wonder if it's a jibe at how I magicked our breakup back in Junior year, forcing him to go along with it unknowingly. Before I can say anything, Daniel sits down and points at Marco.

"He'll turn back to human, here shortly. I'm guessing it's almost time," Daniel says.

Marco's tiger form is daunting and beautiful all at the same time. His muscles move in sleek patterns along his form. He shivers when he crouches, and the shifting is instantaneous. I stand up and turn around to give Marco privacy because he is entirely naked.

"Um . . . I'll go pull together some lunch or something."

Marco laughs. "Sounds good, Willow. See you when I'm dressed."

I hear both of them laughing as I leave. I try to

shake my thoughts of Daniel and his stone reaction to the birds.

At the top of the stairs, my back pocket buzzes. I pull out my cell phone and see Sabine on a video call. Closing my bedroom door, I sigh and sit on my bed.

"I was calling to give you an update, but by the look on your face, something is going on there. Tell me?"

I unload everything from Cross and Quinn about confidential information, the birds in the yard, along with Daniel's strange reaction.

Sabine doesn't say a word, and I wonder if we lost our connection because her face looks frozen on the screen.

"Sabine?"

"I'm digesting. I called to tell you, I purchased a new home in Terra and have moved all the worthwhile items from MacKinnon Manor. Seems so inconsequential now."

"Not true. You bought a home?"

Am I surprised by her news? Did I think she would live here in my father's house? Do I see myself living here long term?

Sabine's face lights up, her eyes widen, and her hands move as she talks.

"I did! I found a large enough estate to house all of MacKinnon Manor staff. We didn't discuss it but, it's not in Massachusetts. It's on the side of a mountain in Arizona, of all places."

"Arizona?"

"I know, but there is something about this place. The view is new for me, the desert landscape. I also feel a pull that magick is strong here."

"I can't wait to see it."

"How about now?"

Sabine smiles and flips the camera around and walks around the house. It's light and bright. So many windows and light walls. Sabine is right. I see the pull because the view is overlooking a valley. The pep in her voice as she describes the various rooms and where everything will go makes any weight of the day seem lighter.

At the end of the tour, Sabine sits down.

"So, what do you think? Would you want to stay here?"

Yes, I want to scream, but I hold back my ten-year-old-self enthusiasm.

"Is this going to be a hub for Terra?"

"Maybe, but it's not my intention. I have on the second floor an entire suite area, if you'd like it. You could split your time there and—"

"I'd love to move there," I spit out before I think too much. I need a change of scenery. I don't want to be in this house alone. There is nothing keeping me here in Chepstow.

Sabine's voice hitches with excitement. The more we talk about it, the more excited I'm getting. Its forward movement. She will arrange a few staff members to help me pack. We don't talk about the inevitability of selling this house, but it's on my mind, along with those staying here.

"Sabine, before we get off the call. Do you have any ideas about these birds? Do you think Daniel or one of my friends are involved?"

A chill runs up my spine thinking about it. It's like I've betrayed my friendships thinking this way.

"I don't know Daniel the way you do, but people change. Motivations and circumstances change. Be mindful and take everything at face value. There is no reason to take risks with yourself or those around you."

She's right. I need to see things as they are now, not as how they once were.

Sabine continues, "With all that is going on, the collapse of a magical realm. It's frightening for everyone. We are fortunate that our displacement is one of privilege."

I can't get Sabine's last statement out of my head.

I know it may not be much, but maybe I can use the money left to me by my father's will or even this house to help those who have no home. I make a voice memo to myself to call the estate attorney on Monday.

CHAPTER 10

I dress nicer today in anticipation of Emily coming over. Daniel is sitting on my bed reading one of my books when I come out of my bathroom.

"Whatca got there?"

Daniel laughs. "Actually, I'm not sure, but it's fairly entertaining." He waves the paperback in my direction before setting it back on my nightstand. It's one of my sci-fi books.

Duke's ears perk up, and I pet his head on my way to my closet to grab my hoodie.

"Want to go outside before Emily gets here?" Daniel asks.

"Nah, I'm just a little cold today in the house, and besides, this is my comfy hoodie," I laugh.

"Oh, right, I forgot you had classifications for hoodies," Daniel teases and follows me down the hall toward the back stairs. "What is it, comfy, outdoor, workout, and what am I forgetting?"

"Duh, it's the formal hoodie."

His smile reaches his eyes. "Right, right . . . formal. Now, let me ask this, when is a hoodie considered formal?"

I laugh before I can answer. The alert from the enchantments around the house notifies us that Emily is here. It's like vibration to the wrist that tingles. But it signals more than once, which is odd. We both pass by the kitchen toward the foyer.

Knock-knock.

I open the door to find not only Emily, but Lucy and Coral.

"Hey." Did my voice just lift two octaves? This is unexpected, seeing Lucy and Coral.

Cross will not be happy about this, and what's more surprising is Emily said nothing about bringing others.

"I know it's been a while. We were all together and thought we'd join Emily coming over. Is that okay?" Lucy smiles easily and walks in as if nothing has changed over the last six months.

"Um . . . sure." I open the door wider and notice that Daniel is no longer behind me. So, I'm going through this alone, I guess.

Coral's eyes and head turning each way, surveying

the foyer as she enters the house. I guess she hasn't ever been inside my house before.

"I'm thinking of a movie in the entertainment room to just hang. Soda and popcorn?" I ask.

"Okay, but I have dibs because we still have not watched Pretty in Pink yet," Emily says, and Lucy groans.

"I was thinking something a little more from this decade. What is it with you and the eighties lately?" Lucy jabs at Emily as they walk up the stairs, familiar with the location of the entertainment room.

Coral slowly walks to the bottom of the stairs. "You've got a beautiful home, Willow. Thanks for letting me crash."

We've been through a lot together, with phantoms attacking our class and graduation, so I no longer look at us as opposing teams. I'm not sure we are on the same team, but since we have the same friend group, it seems like I should let it go.

"So, you've been hanging out with Lucy more," I say as we walk up the stairs.

Coral shrugs. "We've been friends for a long time. Although, of course, her parents and mine have been hanging out more, yeah, I guess."

We walk into the entertainment room, and Emily and Lucy laugh and look at the touchpad that we use as a remote control.

"Yes, let's watch it!" Emily smiles.

"Absolutely not. I say we watch this." She points to some romantic comedy.

I come up behind them and see Emily has chosen the newest hero flick. They both look at me with wide eyes. I respond, "I don't really care either way."

Coral gives the final vote, and the romantic comedy plays. The popcorn machine begins to turn and heat to cook the popcorn. I grab water and sodas out of the small fridge behind the reclining couches with Emily.

"Glad to see you and Lucy are getting along," I say to Emily under my breath.

"Yeah, it's definitely gotten better. How's Daniel? I recognize he's staying out of the way. It's a double whammy with Lucy and Coral both being here."

I shrug, but she's right. Could he have more ex-girlfriends under one roof?

"By the way, thanks for the heads up on that one."

"Sorry, lately I've been caving to Lucy's whims and trying to be more supportive. And Daniel?"

"He's doing well, training with Cross and staying busy. He might as well be a Guardian."

Emily's eyes light up, and she smiles. "Cross is here, still?"

"I'm sure he'll see you before you all leave. Is it better? Have you guys talked?"

"We have had little opportunity." She shrugs. "He's

probably still standing his ground like a testosterone idiot."

"Does he have a good reason?"

She shrugs and shakes her head. "It's just the way it is. I can't give up on my family and what she needs right now." She reveals nothing further. It sure seems like Emily is giving up a lot for Lucy, including her own happiness.

When the popcorn stops, I gather two large bowls and fill them up, and Emily carries the drinks and napkins. By the time we sit, the movie is already kicking off with the two central characters meeting.

I stare at the screen but don't really pay attention to the movie because Rhydian comes to my mind. Was a romantic movie really the best idea? I wonder if he's been talking with Quinn and Cross. I'm sure they would tell me if anything was wrong.

Before I know it, the movie is about halfway over. I excuse myself and go to the bathroom. Out in the hall, Marco pulls me into his room, and Cross and Quinn are sitting on the bed, making it look like a twin. Daniel is missing from the room.

"What the heck?" I stammer. They stare at me with their arms folded over their chests.

"They need to leave. There were more birds at the perimeter, and we've taken care of them, but it was more this time," Cross says.

"It could be the increase of magick users with

Emily? Also, Lucy is part valkyrie, so who knows," Quinn says.

"Okay, the movie is almost over, then I'll say I have to do something or whatever."

"I can help with that excuse." Cross smiles.

"Where is Daniel?"

"He's hiding out in his room," Marco replies.

This is strange, and I wonder if Emily is aware someone might track her and Lucy. But if she is knowledgeable, would she have come here? Surely, she would have said something to me. I sit down and nudge her when she eats the last popcorn in our bowl and smiles at me like a Cheshire cat.

"You didn't want anymore, right?" Emily says lightheartedly and drags her finger on the bottom of the bowl to get the last of the white cheddar powder topping that had settled to the bottom of the bowl.

"Something is going on. Be careful when you're in public, okay?" I say under my breath.

Her eyebrows pinch together, and she nods and turns back to the big screen.

When the movie ends, the lights, which are on an automated timer, brighten, and I stand. Lucy is stretching and yawning.

"Another movie?" Coral asks.

"Actually, I'm tired suddenly. I hate to be a buzzkill, but I have plans later. I'll need to get back home," Lucy responds.

I don't need an excuse after all.

"Yeah, me too. I need to do a few things tonight," Emily says.

Coral fidgets with her hands. "Hey, Willow, where is your bathroom?" I point her down the hall, hoping that the guys have dispersed.

We are cleaning up and turning everything off when Coral pops in the doorway. "Okay, ready to leave."

Down the stairs, Coral is lingering as Emily, Lucy, and I say our goodbyes. Emily and Lucy have odd looks on their faces when Coral approaches me. She grabs my hand and clasps it in her own. Then I feel something: a piece of paper.

"I know we didn't always see eye to eye in high school, but thank you for allowing me to crash with you all this afternoon," Coral says to me. Her eyes are intense and staring directly at me as she pushes for me to palm the paper from her hand to my hand.

"No worries, all in the past," I respond. Following her lead, I cup the paper in my hand and press my thumb over it, so it's secure when I bring her into a hug. "No worries, Coral, I'm glad we're putting things behind us."

I went too far. She is stiff as she steps back from me. I laugh. "Sorry, too soon?" I quickly slide it into my back pocket.

She laughs and says, "Yeah, maybe. See ya."

Lucy follows her out the door, but not before giving me a quick hug and reaching for my empty hands.

"I'm glad we had today," Lucy says.

When I shut the door, I look out the side window and watch them leave in Lucy's car. Coral is in the back seat with her arms folded and her lips pursed. Lucy is red-faced and talking loudly.

"What was that?" Daniel says, and I jump at his voice.

"Dang, sorry, I didn't mean to scare you."

Cross, Quinn, and Marco are behind Daniel.

"That was a little too easy, and what was with Lucy?" Quinn asks.

It's a good question. She seemed unhappy to have Coral and me not be at odds with one another. But, also, what's this crap about, glad we had today? Something is off, very off.

"Did Coral give you something?" Daniel asks.

Keeping my composure together, I shrug with my hand in my back pocket over the paper. "No." I shake my head.

He makes light of it but keeps his eyes stay on me before he and Marco walk away.

I usher Cross and Quinn into the formal living room. Touching Cross's wristband, I say, "Do that cone of silence thingy."

"Liar. She gave you something," Cross whispers in

a sly grin as he secures the room.

I pull the note from my back pocket and hold the small, folded paper in my hand.

"Coral passed me this and didn't want Lucy or Emily to see it. She was even shielding it from Daniel since he was right next to us."

Quinn cradles my hand. "I'm not sure you . . . it could be cursed or something?"

"It's not cursed. It is Coral, and she owes me twice for saving her life. Besides, she must have just written it when she was in the bathroom."

Cross points. "Well, yer just gonna stare at it?"

He's right. I'm staring at it. I am careful to open it, the ink is smearing, it's dark and wet. Part of it gets on my fingertips.

"This is blood," Quinn says.

I open the last fold and read it in a quiet voice. "Don't trust them. Lucy, Daniel, or Emily."

Cross's voice gets louder. "What the hell? Tis the girl serious or playing with ya?"

Coral isn't the type to play games like this. It must be serious because she wouldn't go through all this trouble to hand me a note in secret and no less in the blood that is probably hers.

I stare at them and say, "No, this is serious."

"Do you trust what she wrote?" Quinn asks.

I don't want to. They are my friends, my good friends. Although Coral and I haven't been friends in the past, we have an understanding now. Whereas my friends are acting odd. Emily has never given me any doubt of her loyalty to my friendship or the crown. She's always been by my side, and I by hers. Lucy is a wild card since her outrage at prom when she turned Daniel into an einherjar warrior.

"I don't want to, but we need to be careful."

"This is bullshit! Daniel!" Cross yells.

I grab Cross's arm and say under my breath, "Don't out Coral."

The room is still secure. Daniel didn't hear Cross, and he realizes it when he taps his wrist cuff.

"Listen, don't go all hot-headed on Daniel yet," I say.

Cross's jaw is clenched.

Quinn holds the note. "Coral could be in danger. We need to be very careful."

"Daniel! Marco! Where you guys at?"

Marco is the one who responds. "Kicking my ass gaming."

"Seriously, can you be stealth at all?" I ask.

Cross turns, with Quinn on his heels, back to me. "Yeah, it's a 101 course at academy training." Cross's eye roll makes me want to smack him.

"That's it! You don't say two words about any of this." I put the paper back into my pocket.

"We won't. I promise." Quinn nudges Cross. "We will need to report in later to the commander. Who, I expect, will say Daniel needs to move out immediately. He can't be here."

How will I explain that to Daniel or Emily?

"Right, but keeping a watch on him here gives us a tactical advantage, possibly. I say we put some tracers and coms in his room," Cross adds.

It's come to this already. Spying on Daniel in the house? Shit.

I agree with Cross and Quinn.

In my room, I pull out my phone and find a text from an unknown number.

It's true.

I text back.

Who is this?

I wait and there is no response, but there is this feeling in my gut: it's Coral. I try one more text.

I can help you.

I wait for several minutes, but there is no response.

CHAPTER 11

Cross looks satisfied as he takes a second bite of the greasy pan-fried burgers, he's made for us. Wide-eyed, I pick up mine and compress it to take a healthy bite.

"Am I right?" he asks, waiting as he swallows his mouth full.

He's so right. It melts right into my mouth. The gooey cheese he pushed into the middle of the beef is absolute heaven. Cross got into a Food TV marathon over the past day, and it's really paid off.

"I'm sure glad I made two for everyone because there is no way I'm not eating another one."

I laugh and realize that there won't be any leftovers.

Quinn walks in and gets a burger and fries for himself. "So, what burger did you go with, Cross?"

"Rachel Ray's cheese in the middle combo."

"Excellent," Marco and Daniel say in unison, joining us in the kitchen.

I'm sitting at a table with all of them and realizing Cross and Quinn are not only Guardians or my friends. They are my family. Living here in the house and us doing so much together has been a much-needed distraction. Between the silence of Rhydian and the second-guessing of Coral's note about Lucy, Daniel, and Emily, my brain is on its last circuit, and it's all I can do to hold it together. Who knows, except that Cross is one helluva cook.

"So, are we playing *Call of Duty* tonight?" Quinn nods to Daniel.

Daniel easily fits into Cross and Quinn's groove. It's like he's a guardian himself, over and above being an einherjar warrior.

Cross has learned nothing on Daniel, which I hope stays that way. Of course, we're probably overreacting. I hate this need to be secretive, but that note is a like question that hangs in the air.

They continue chatting about video games and various online professional players I know nothing about.

"Willow, do you want to hang and check it out?" Marco asks me.

I smile, fully knowing it's a pity question, because

video games are out of my league, at least at the level they are chatting about.

"Nah, I think I'll hang about reading and maybe catch up on some other stuff."

After dinner, they all head to the spot they've carved out in the entertainment room. I make my way to my father's office. In this house, I will always see this as his office. I walk past the desk and run my hand across the slick wood and open the hidden doorway from the bookcase to reveal the solitary coven room. The lamps light the way in the short, dark hallway to an oval room with an overstuffed chair and footstool. I flip my fingers, and the floor lamp illuminates with the fireplace that is shared with the office. There is a table with a mortar and pestle. Dried herbs and other liquids in glasses line the shelf above the table.

My father showed me this room when I learned about my heritage. Being here is like a warm hug from my parents. It no longer brings tears to my eyes. I breathe in the air and the lingering scent of sage that I burned yesterday.

Plopping my butt into the overstuffed paisley chair, I hook my legs over the armrest. On the ottoman is our family book of shadows. I lay it in my lap and trace my fingers on the raised covered crest design engrained beneath a triquetra. It wasn't long ago that I was learning what a triquetra was from my uncle. I've learned so much since then.

My phone buzzes and shakes my hip with a notification. Pulling it from my pocket, I see it's Cross.

Got to check in with Eoin. Will be back soon.

Willow: *Why, what's going on?*

Cross: *Check-in on a family nearby.*

Willow: *Is Quinn going too?*

Cross: *Yeah.*

Willow: *Want some company? When are you leaving?*

Cross: *Just me & Quinn. We'll leave in about 15 min.*

Staring at my family's book of shadows, I open the front page and flip through it casually. So many of the pages appear to be empty. It's deceiving though, because as I scan through the pages, they fill in. I stop midway and stare at the pages with newly formed ink. The ownership of the crown and family lineage. I've seen it before, but I watch it unfold. My picture is under my grandfather, Harkin MacKinnon, the Wiccan King. He followed my great grandfather, Thurmond MacKinnon, and prior to that was my great-great-grandmother, Gabrielle Baudelaire. They based the lineage on power and arranged marriages, and they held it for hundreds of years in my family. My mother should be here, but she isn't on this page, only those who have held the Wiccan Crown in Edayri. The script of my name appears, *Willow Sola Warrington.*

With something so powerful, why do I feel so useless? I feel like a schoolgirl under house arrest, a punishment to keep me safe, even though I am one of the most powerful Wiccans. I resent that I have to follow the decisions of the legion council. Yet, I'm the one who made it and gave it power. I didn't want Edayri to be ruled as a monarchy. So, why is there a voice in my head that taunts and pushes me?

The words morph on the page, the ink dissolving in the page's cotton fibers, then reappearing.

Concentrate and ask again.

I touch the words. I should be involved, right?

Without a doubt.

Then why aren't I?

Reply hazy; try again.

I sit up and let out a huff in frustration. The book is correct. I haven't been involved and can't sit by the sidelines anymore. Same with Rhydian. He can't ignore me forever. I need more, even if it's over. Enough is enough.

Yes.

I laugh.

"Oh, I agree," I say to no one, just the empty room and the book of shadows. But, with Rhydian on my mind, do I dare ask the question? Despite knowing some answers from Evan . . . can the broken blood vow be forgiven of its commitment? I doubt an eight-ball type response will help me, but maybe—just maybe the book can point me in the . . .

Without a doubt.

The book's pages turn, and I stare in amazement when the words scroll across the page. A blood vow to the crown. I can't read the words fast enough, and the sentences soak into my mind like an already wet sponge. I'm not comprehending what I'm reading. I stop and breathe and re-read the second paragraph for the third time.

If the giver breaks a vow, the recipient may absolve the giver of the vow, should the connection not be in treason to the Goddess herself. No blood vow should be taken lightly; the giver's death is imminent upon the recipient's death. The Goddess may have cause to strip a vow if haste is made for the crown or in sabotage to the crown of the Goddess herself.

Can I forgive the blood vow myself? Am I the embodiment of the Goddess? Evan said I am, but is he right? Am I?

Concentrate and ask again.

Fuck! I'm tired of this ache, this pain because of Rhydian and me being apart. Is he punishing me because I helped him break the vow to free him? Is it a pride and loyalty thing? Is the Goddess punishing me? This is uber fucked up!

It is certain.

Geez, thanks for the support. My eyes are heavy thinking about Rhydian. I miss him, and my heart hurts. Maybe I should forget it like he has. I don't want to hate him, but my resentment builds like a disease with every passing day. It's been almost three weeks.

I think about kissing him, laughing, and his smirk. His hand is holding mine. The warmth that comforts me. Him seeing me for the first time, his all-business warrior face. Us grappling on the training mat. His face when I came down the stairs in my prom dress.

"Willow! Willow! Where are you?"

"Hum?" I rub my eyes, and Daniel is coming into the coven room. His face is pale. I stand and go to him, and the book falls to the floor with a loud thump.

Outlook is not so good.

"What happened?"

"We got a text from Cross. We got to go help them."

I follow Daniel out of the coven room, and Marco is pacing back and forth.

"Do you know where they are?" I ask.

Daniel hands me his phone with an address that's three towns over. We can't drive there and get there quickly. I will need to transport all three of us there.

"Are we sure they need us? Daniel, they were clear before they left—to stay here." Marco stops pacing. "I mean, you were talking with Lucy a minute ago."

"Really? You've seen the text . . ." Holding his

phone, Daniel reads it aloud. " 'Could use some backup, put that training to work.' Then the address. You're overthinking it."

Usually Cross sends simple text messages. Maybe I'm overthinking it.

"I don't feel a shift or a rift in the air. We could pop over. I know generally where this is."

"Yes, we can't wait."

Daniel stands next to me, and I hold out my hand. There is a sensation, a connection when our skin touches. He is excited. An opportunity to be out of the house. Marco is slower, reaches for my free hand. I concentrate on the address, and the push of air surrounds us. It's risky transporting.

Holding both Marco and Daniel's hands, we land with little effect under cover of the dark trees in the backyard of a massive house. The dense cloud cover makes it hard to see the house. It doesn't look like anyone is inside. There is no light anywhere.

"Are you sure we are in the right place?" Marco asks.

Daniel nods before speaking. "Oh yeah, this is the house."

How would he know? Before I can ask, there is a loud crack and a blinding light that shatters all the windows. Marco and I duck and cover our ears. Daniel is running toward the house.

"I guess this is the right place then."

I follow Marco, and we make our way into the house but lose sight of Daniel. It's too quiet. We are in a mud room that leads to a longer hallway. The hallway leads to an open floor plan that is completely wrecked. Furniture tossed, items on the floor all over, and pictures barely hanging on.

"Cross. Quinn. Where are you?" I yell. My magick surfaces quickly, the hum radiating all over me.

This is wrong. Something is wrong here.

"Willow."

It's Cross's voice. It's faint, and he's coughing somewhere to the left of me. There is a staircase in the middle of the space, and I see a woman laying head toward the bottom of the stairs, eyes open, but there is no life there. Marco goes to the woman and shakes his head after checking for a pulse.

There are holes in the ceiling with burn marks everywhere. Water is dribbling down a wall in the center.

"Cross?" I call out.

I barely make out his hulking body near an overturned soft. As I get closer to him, I hesitate because he looks like a wounded animal that may strike. He has burn marks all over him. He takes a few seconds to recognize me.

"Willow, over here now!" Cross commands. He's

leaning over something small. I see others in my periphery unmoving on the ground, but the one Cross is over and protecting is a little girl.

Her slight frame is still, and she has blood all around her. I reach to her and my magick flows instantly. Her skin brightens, and she gives a weak cough.

"Shit, Quinn!" Daniel says. He's on the opposite side.

As I stand, Cross grabs my hand to stop me. His shaking courses through me.

"Cross. What happened?"

"It was an ambush," Cross replies.

He won't look at me. Then his shoulders heave and his eyes snap to mine. "She was the only one who stood a chance."

The little girl sits up and starts crying.

Marco runs into the room and slides to a stop surveying the damage.

"He's gone, Willow. Gone."

"What does that mean, Cross?" I look back at Daniel, who is only staring at the familiar shoes and pants that were in my house a few minutes ago.

Quinn.

I listen to Cross explain that he and Quinn came to this house on the routine check-in with this Wiccan family. When they transported in, the hunters were already there.

His voice breaks, but he continues, "Quinn was calling it in when lightning came and—I was a target in the room and . . ." His voice hitches. "But Quinn. He pushed me out of the way, and he was—"

I can't process this right now. Quinn. Oh Goddess, Quinn. I can't comprehend what Cross is saying. It's Marco's voice that takes me out of my head.

"Murdered."

"It should have been me," he says.

Cross's heavy-set shoulders bob with his head down. I reach out to him. He flinches.

"Are we safe here?" Marco asks.

"We have to get out of here, if they come back . . ." Daniel stops short, still staring at Quinn on the ground.

"I've called in. The legion council representatives for refugees and other Guardians are coming because of the mass casualties. Let them come back, I will—" Cross turns from us.

I reach for the little girl, picking her up to hold her. She clutches my neck and buries her face in my shoulder. Her tears and mine mix. I rock her in the swing of my hips to help comfort her, but maybe I was doing it more for me. I can't go to Quinn and see him there, lying on the floor.

Am I sure I'm not still sleeping, and this is a nightmare? I don't know how the time passes, but I track the movements of everyone. Including Guardians' and council members' arrival.

My heart squeezes when the legion council representative takes the little girl from my arms.

"It'll be okay," I whisper to her when her little hand reaches for mine.

Do I believe that?

All I can think about is the burn marks all over the house. Lightning, a signature of a valkyrie. I know others must think the same thing. Although a Wiccan can do the same damage, why would they turn on their own in this way? Why would any magickal being?

I try everything I can to think of what could have done this horrible crime to this family, because I don't want my mind to wander to the note from Coral. The accusations of Lucy, Emily, and Daniel. Daniel led us here. Marco said Daniel was just speaking with Lucy.

The grief is heavy in this house, from everyone I see. Guardians surveying the house and removing four bodies, including Quinn's. But it doesn't look right on Daniel. It seems rehearsed and disingenuous. I want to grab him by the collar.

"Cross, when did you text Daniel?" I ask.

Daniel is a good fifteen feet away, but he hears me and turns. His stare is holding mine. He lied.

"What?" Cross shakes his head.

Eoin stomps into the house. Daniel's eyes move to him.

"Yeah, maybe, Willow, I might have," Cross says.

Daniel turns away and goes with Marco outside. They are being driven back to my house.

I barely recall Eoin talking with me and Cross. Cross gave a blow by blow on the hit. He didn't know exactly how many hunters were involved, but he suspected ten surrounded the house. It was firepower they hadn't seen yet on at this magnitude. Eoin was all business, but his voice was louder and more authoritative. He knew Quinn died tonight, but he doesn't show it.

The focus comes back the moment Eoin shakes me. Before I'm enveloped in a hug that is stiff from Eoin. I speak, but he cuts me off.

"Sabine is outside in a vehicle with a Guardian to drive you home. Cross will need to go back with me."

"No."

"Willow . . ."

"Cross needs to stay with me. This is too close to my home. He's a Royal Guardian—"

"Fine. Cross leaves with you."

Eoin turns toward a young Guardian, barking an order. I walk out the front door and find Cross in an SUV with Sabine in the passenger seat.

In the car, it is quiet. Sabine didn't talk, and neither did Cross. We were together but silent in our sadness. The ride felt short as we pull into the tree covered entryway of the driveway toward my father's house.

The Guardian who was driving us parked and turned off the engine.

"I will stay outside tonight, with another Guardian soon. Please get some rest."

"Thank you," Sabine says before leading me in the front door.

Cross closes the heavy front door, and I jump at the sound.

"Oh, sweetheart. I can't believe this happened." Sabine hugs me by her side.

Marco is at the top of the stairs.

"Where is Daniel?" I ask.

"He left as soon as we got here. Said he had to see Emily and would be back later."

I want to say something to Cross, but I don't know what I think I know. He said he texted Daniel, right? I can talk with Daniel later. Daniel wasn't there when this happened, anyway. He was with me and Marco.

Cross passes Marco, making his way up the stairs slowly.

"I'm staying here tonight. Do you need anything? How about tea?" Sabine asks.

"Maybe? But I can't move. I don't want to think about Quinn—and how—he . . ." The burst of my lung's pulses with each heaving cry because I can't form a sentence.

Sabine and I sit on the formal stiff couch because it's closest to the foyer. She holds me and we both cry until I am taken upstairs to my bed and covered with a blanket.

CHAPTER 12

There's no way, absolutely no way, I'm staying in this house. I'm going to Quinn's funeral. Over the last three days, the hunters have killed over twenty Wiccans alone. This group of people, these hunters, who are slaughtering anyone with magickal abilities, is a priority threat. The legion council is holding funerals in mass in the realm of New Haven. New Haven is a refugee holding post outside of Edayri that seems unaffected by the rifts, or at least that is what Sabine and Eoin have said. It should be safe, where the funerals are, plus if anything happens, my magick and training are an asset. I keep rehearsing this in my head, walking down the stairs dressed in black with my long overcoat.

"Ya think yer gonna get by me? I know what ya think. Hell, I want to go too, but we can't. Willow, and the last thing I need to do"—his voice a whisper when he looks away—"is failing, again."

Cross doesn't look at me. He's staring at the floor.

"I believe the instructions were to stick with me. And guess what, I'm leaving. So, if you want to continue your assigned duty, you will need to follow me."

Marco is in black slacks, a gray shirt, and a dark jacket. He shrugs his shoulders at Cross. "I've known her a lot longer than you have. When she sets her mind to do something, especially tied to a friend, it's gonna happen."

I can't help but weakly smile at Marco. I hate we are here in this situation.

"This is nice and all, but you don't have a pass or transporting ordinance for the funeral. If we transport, we're shooting in the dark."

I pull out of my pocket a glowing paper with the coordinates flashing in a sequence of alphanumeric code. It wasn't hard to get from Sabine without her knowledge.

"Well, aren't you the little thief," Cross says. His smirk is approval enough we are going to the funeral.

"No, just resourceful."

And then Marco adds, "In a stubborn-headed, beyond-belief way."

We wait while Cross changes his clothes in happy defeat.

We each hold on to the card with our thumbs and forefingers. Marco hooks his arm into mine on one side and Cross to the other. I'm a magickal battery. This was the only way we can get there without coordinates in the Guardian wristband together. Calling to my magick, the familiar hum rises to the surface, and I attach it to the code in the card that guides us in transport. It isn't smooth transport; we get jolted, and my shoulder knocks into Cross's muscled arm. It feels like a running stop as we land in New Haven. The greenway strip is holding the mass funeral. Others are transporting around us, and it conceals us in the crowd.

Cross like me has a hood on his coat, and we pull them up to obscure ourselves to those around us. No one would recognize Marco unless we run into Sabine or Eoin.

My heart aches for Eoin. Quinn was so happy being more public in his relationship with Eoin. My mind replays the memory of Quinn feeling comfortable enough to tell me about it after prom dress shopping. I didn't realize, at that time, it was Eoin until we were fighting at MacKinnon Manor. I can't think about it, or my eyes will pool with tears.

Cross pulls me out of my reverie. "Everyone's walking this way, go."

Marco and I follow Cross through the crowd.

The dull ache of my heart twists, Rhydian. He still

hasn't responded to me, and most likely he's here for his best friend. Will we see each other? I clench my fists and release them while steadying my breath. I'm not here for Rhydian. I'm here for Quinn and Cross, and all of us who are grieving. Isn't that what a funeral is, anyway? It's not for those gone, it's for those left behind.

The legion council has a stage set up in front of the new Hallowed Hall on the outskirts of a refugee camp. There is a podium and several chairs on the stage. I see her bright hair flowing behind her as she walks up onto the stage. It's Sabine. I glance to the side to avoid her spotting me in the crowd. Abigail is on stage, and sitting next to her is Evan. He's looking straight out like a statue. I wedge between Marco and myself behind a large man, so he obscures us. Knowing Evan, he probably knows I'm here with his gift of knowing future events, but maybe not.

A member of the legion council at the podium taps on a microphone that booms their voice over the crowd. The noise of those gathered quiets when Aren approaches the podium.

"It is with great sadness that we gather today to mourn the loss of several in our community. We are fortunate to have found temporary homes in New Haven and Terra. We grieve for our lost lands and homes, but most of all, we feel the loss of our fellow Edayrians. May we honor our ancestors in our final resting place and carry those we've lost to the home-land." The surrounding people are watching move-ments on the stage and podium. At the sound of the horn, all the Wiccans say together, "As above and as below, blessed be."

A new member of the legion council reads the names of those who have died. Cross moves to the side, away from my eyesight, giving us space, but I know he's here. This is horrible, a mass funeral. I try to be as inconspicuous as possible, watching those around me, some staring ahead, seeing the names magickally carved into a pillar behind those on the stage. Others lean on their loved ones with tear-stained faces, and their eyes cast down to the ground. The cyclical rumination about Quinn and the fact he's no longer with us is a pain I know all too well. I've cried, hit things, blamed myself, and let the sorrow wash over me only a few days ago. Right now, I feel numb.

The ache I want to feel—is missing.

Marco steps in front of me before a person in the gray hooded coat turns and lowers his hood.

"You've got some nerve . . ." Marco says.

I barely touch Marco's shoulder, and he moves.

His name, it's on the tip of my tongue, but I can't speak. I look into his stormy ocean eyes. He's doing the same, assessing my face. His eyebrows pinch together, and his lips part. I'd almost forgot how his lip quirks to the left before he speaks. My heart isn't twisting in pain, but my pulse is rushing through me. He's calm, as if we just saw each other. Rhydian doesn't seem like a broken shell of a man. He looks like himself.

"I thought you weren't coming," Rhydian says.

"I'm sorry to ruin that for you," I reply, trying to keep my tone even.

He shakes his head and turns around, away from me. I can't believe him. One sentence that punches me in the gut. That's it? That is all he's going to say?

He was hoping not to see me. I swallow the bitter medicine that he is, in fact, avoiding me. I've had enough. He will not ignore me! I grab his arm before he's entirely lost to me in a crowd of people.

"Are you fucking kidding me? That is all you're going to say to me? Well, I've got a lot to say to you, Rhydian."

His mouth opens as if he's about to say something, but he doesn't. He looks like a puppet, his jaw opening and closing.

"Am I that intimidating? You can't say whatever it is you're going to say? I know Quinn means more to you than me, and I'm sure he's happy you are here, but you're late! You're very fucking late."

His exhale was audible. And he reaches for my elbow and leads me off to the side of the crowd. No one is taking notice as we slip by quietly, despite the rage in my head. He turns to me when we are far enough away from the greenbelt of the crowd and near a gravel pathway that enters through dense woods.

"I don't know what to say to you. Everything I needed to say, I said at MacKinnon Manor that day. I just am not ready."

Ready? What the hell is he talking about?

He continues and looks around me before meeting my eyes.

"I feel if I say it, it's more real, and I'm drowning in disappointments and failures. I found my mother. She passed away only three years ago. So, I had a lovely conversation at her gravesite. Another failure, one I can't even press my father about or yell at him for. And I have to come to terms with the fact that the man who raised me was also willing to kill me. Last, one of my very best friends died. I wasn't there—"

He pushes his hand through his hair, and he's looking everywhere except at me.

I want to yell, but I can't. Aware of what his father did and was prepared to do. I did not know about his mother. We both have so much loss in our lives, both of our parents have died. My fist releases, and my pulse steadies.

"So, when do you leave? Are you only here for the funeral?"

He takes a step back from me.

"I've been back with the Guardians for the last month. They kept it confidential. It was an agreement I had with Eoin. I needed to be a soldier again, with purpose. I needed the routine, the missions, the direction."

I can't hear the rest of what he is saying, just the fact that he's been here for a month. That wasn't long after graduation. He must've found out about his mother earlier. He was nearby to me, and he actively avoided me. Abby said it's not like him to run away. Did he hide it from his sister to? My breathing is getting harder. I can't hear what he says. I'm shaking my head, trying to clear the preaching thoughts in my mind.

It was the blood vow; that's what tied him to me.

None of it was real.

Why do I continue to hurt? Why am I still mourning us?

"Why are you running from me?" I didn't realize I asked until he answered.

"What? I'm not running, I'm—"

"Are you? What about the damage and the hurt you've left in your wake?" I raise my voice, and he flinches in his shoulders. "Tell me I'm right."

Tullen is coming toward us and allows Rhydian to avoid my question.

"Hey, Eoin is looking for you, Rhydian." Tullen

looks at me before saying, "He knows you're here. He spotted Cross and Marco. It's okay, although I wouldn't make it a habit to not tell Sabine what you're doing."

Rhydian walks away from us, and I want to follow. I need to follow, but I resign myself to throwing my hands in the air.

"Tullen, this is so messed up! He won't—he doesn't even care."

"Willow, that's not true."

I spy Rhydian and Cross in a quick hug and talking. "I just don't understand why he won't even talk to me. Am I that awful? Did it all just evaporate? Were all those feelings just part of the unwanted blood vow?"

Tullen blocks my view so that he's in front of me. "Absolutely not. Rhydian is punishing himself in his own private atonement. You feel that ache when he's not near, right? His is 100-fold, and it's a pain, an ache that he wants because he's so—for lack of a better word, ashamed. For a man like Rhydian, loyalty is everything, and he broke his—"

"But not of his own awareness. It was his father who manipulated everyone and—"

"Yes, his father. A man he loved. He's reconciling a lot about who he is. You've got to understand that the blood vow you helped him break pulled at everything he believes is at the core of who he is."

My arms shake and I clench my hands. "I didn't have a choice. There was no other way."

"Willow, you know what it's like to lose loving parents. Can you imagine his scenario, and he lost someone he was falling in love with?"

I want to cry and hit something, listening to Tullen. But he's right. I'm grieving over it and have been for months. But for me, avoiding each other is worse. There is no closure, and it's a sitting ache that haunts me. I can't live like this.

Rhydian is moving from Cross, and Marco is walking away from me. Sabine and Evan are walking toward me at the back of the field.

I'm not done talking to Rhydian. Not done yelling and—my vision waivers as I take my steps toward him in the opposite way of Sabine and Evan. I push through the crowd that is trying to swallow him from my reach.

"Rhydian!" I yell.

He stops, and his head drops, only for a moment before he walks again through groups of people. He is walking away from me again, but this time no good-bye. My steps get faster, and before I know it, I'm running toward him, yelling his name again. That is almost a curse. I grab onto his arm, and when he turns around, it is instantaneous. We need to talk, and I'm transporting us. His lips push together in a line. His eyebrows pinch together. I don't care because it's a mirror of how I feel. The transport pulls and pushes us. My death grip on his arm isn't allowing him to leave, not this time.

The transport pulls us; my magick flares. He pulls my hand from his arm, and when we land, we break apart in darkness. The air leaves from my chest as my ass hits the hard surface. The atmosphere is musty, and my hands feel like I'm touching a chalk-like substance. Clapping my hands, I stand in the darkness. I can't see anything in front of me.

"Willow! Shit. Where did you transport us?"

His voice is close to me. Holding my hand in front of my face, I barely see it. The smell of the stale air is unfamiliar.

"I don't know, obviously this isn't my home in Chepstow, that's for sure."

I call to my magick and it hums to life in the various patterns and designs on my skin, along with the hovering crown above my head. Rhydian is close behind me. I turn to face him. He hits his wrist cuff, and light surrounds us when he tosses an illuminating stone to a red dirt floor.

"Goddess, Willow, where the hell are we?"

Is it a hole? The sides look like the red dirt ground but are carved, arching overhead and far above.

"It must be a cave? I'm not sure."

He paces. "What were you thinking? Have you lost your mind? We didn't have a pathway, a time point—we could be anywhere!" His voice is rising, and so is the pressure in my chest.

His yelling fuels me—finally, communication.

"If you would have turned and faced me, talked to me. I wouldn't have resorted to this." I stomp.

"I had nothing left to say!" His lips are tight, and his face is stone. The ridge of his brow bone gives a shadow over his face that is intimidating.

"Well, I do!"

He mockingly gestures to me. "Well, did you ever think I don't want to hear it?"

"You're a fucking coward then, because I'm not done. Ignoring me does not make me disappear." My voice carries, but it doesn't stop me. "You left, and your pain is mine! Did you know that? You left and that pain you feel, the one you enjoy punishing yourself with, that it also punishes me?"

He's not surprised by this, his face still stone. I can't stand this. All I wanted was closure, and now all I want to do is smack him.

"You knew! Your silence is deafening!" I yell. With a thrust of my hands, I push the air with my magick and hit him. Did he expect it? He touches his wrist cuff, and his guardian armor extends to cover his body. I don't let it finish before I'm in front of him, and my arm is moving of its own volition with conjured light and air. He jumps to the side, and my magick misses him.

My legs are being swept out from under me, and I quickly rotate to my side. The jolt goes to my mind. If he won't talk to me, at least this is real. I fall into my training. I'm on offense and attacking with my body, arms, and legs, falling into a rhythm that Rhydian easily blocks and deflects. My eyes water in this dance, and I'm blind, but my movements are steady and connecting.

I scream and scream.

Ah!

The echo around me fuels me, and my magick hums, connecting and compounding. I'm bursting with the absence of the ache. His continued rejection.

Rhydian is not striking back. He's only protecting himself. His arms deflect.

I just can't anymore.

My arms fall to my side, and I stop. Heaving, I bend over to catch my breath and wipe my eyes. My magick flows all around my skin. I'm controlling it. My magick is not misfiring. It's working as I intend for it too.

"Willow."

My name is a whisper, and as much as my heart lifts to my name on his lips, I sink.

CHAPTER 13

My wrath, my anger, and my sadness are rolled into one. All I can think about is the comment from Evan; that the blood vow was not something I accepted. The blood vow made was to my father, not directly to me, but for me.

"I can't continue like this. You're dwelling on your own self-pity and suffering, but it is also causing mine! Do you have any idea that our separation causes constant pain to me? You're making me suffer."

His eyes relax, and his lips part.

"Oh, you didn't know that? I figured you wanted me to suffer because I helped to break the blood vow against your commitment, your loyalty to the Guardians, the crown." My voice breaks. "To me!"

He reaches for me, and I step back. "And FYI, the blood vow you made was to my father, not directly with me!" I give a mocking laugh, a moment of courage, and I step forward into his space. "Do you want to hurt me? You've done a magnificent job making me suffer with you. What my pain was of some silly heartbroken girl? What is your goal, Rhydian? Avoidance? Do you think it will all go away if you avoid it? Avoid me?"

He looks everywhere except at me. I move to block him so he has nowhere else to look but at me. This is it, my only chance for him to face me. My heart is thundering in my chest.

"Say it. Spit it out. I do not know what you're feeling, but I can tell you that if you don't speak now, I—"

It comes rushing out of him and feels like a smack in the face.

"I should've never made the blood vow. I would take it back if I could. Is that what you want to hear? Tell me what you want to hear!" he says.

He regrets it all.

He regrets me.

At that moment, it was all I could do not to look away. I pushed him to hear it, and—his kiss is crushing and unexpected. I grasp on to the threads of pain in our lips, the desperation and pull of it, the past that haunts us both. He doesn't push me back. The urgency of his kiss is welcome because it's his, mine, ours. It's a cursed hell we've both been living, and it has to end.

I pull the tether—the ache—the loss. It's tangible, the light and shadow pull. Lifting my hands from him, I direct the magick, the vow, our hurt into a magickal bubble above us.

"We can we be rid of it. A blank slate, a new—"

Rhydian pushes me.

"No!"

Before I can release my magick, I'm pushed off my feet. I stumble to catch my balance before pushing off the wall, and I direct my blast to Rhydian, who easily ducks and rolls to the side.

"Why! Why?" Tears. Pitiful, exhaustible tears threaten to fall. I hate them.

He's in front of me, trying to pull me into him. I don't want to be comforted. The opportunity to be rid of this connection of pain, and he doesn't want that? I can't. I don't want to love him anymore. My tears fall. They are the catalyst. My arms are moving and throwing punches.

He's deflecting my offensive moves, and we are moving in a circle as we used to train in the Guardian gym with Eoin. Yes! It's familiar, and his eyes light up, and my frustration rises at the friendly taunt.

Rhydian is holding back when I kick, and he grabs my leg and hooks me to him. My side is open to him. I take the advantage and hit him with my elbow and come down onto his shoulder. We break apart. He's fighting back.

Isn't that what I've wanted? A reaction. How much will he fight for it? I won't stop. Screw him and his noble, silent suffering.

I conjure my defensive magick in my hand; it lights up, and I toss it toward the contained magick above us. I pulled, but he pushes me, and I miss it. I use the combo Cross taught me, and I hit him, one, two, then spin and sweep his legs—but he grabs my leg and twists me, and I fall on him.

I try to push, but he rolls us, and he's on top of me, breathing hard.

"Get off of me," I say with little conviction.

"No." His eyes are searching. "Willow, I—stop."

The bubble above us dissolves, and the magick settles over each of us. The hurt of the blood vow, because we are near each other, doesn't ache. Goddess, I want to hate him. I cover my face, and the tears stream down my cheeks. My entire body shakes in heaves. It only takes a few seconds. He sits up and helps me do the same. My effort to wipe away my anger with my tears fails.

"I'm sorry, Willow. For how my father manipulated me for my connection with the crown—with you . . . for being so blind. I needed time to sort out my place in all of this. I didn't know that the broken blood vow caused you pain when we're apart, too. I thought it was one-sided. I—"

"It's not the same."

His kiss, the connection we share, is still there with or without a vow that connects us. My finger traces my lips in the rough absence of his.

"Rhydian, I'm a mess of feelings. Are you settled? Are we d—" I can't bring myself to say it. Are we done? It still hurts, but the pain is becoming a familiar friend. I hate this.

"Do you hear that?" he interrupts and turns away from me. His brow furrows.

I slow my breathing to listen and turn toward the faint sound. He's right. We are not alone, maybe a voice? The magick on my skin ripples in patterns.

"It sounds like water. We must be deep in a cavern. It must direct out toward—"

"I think we should go toward the water." I point to my hand. "Look, my magick is moving with it, on my skin."

Rhydian nods, and he picks up the light stone and shines it in front of us. We walk toward the source of the sound. It takes time before it gets louder.

"It sounds almost like there is rushing water? Maybe it's a way out," Rhydian states more than asks.

There is a light string of melodic melodies that float to our ears.

It's fairies.

Rhydian holds the light stone for the glow ahead of us, its soft white light beckoning us forward. The walls give way to an opening that leads to a vast cavern with soaring ceilings and surrounds us like a stadium. The light above is over a cliff-side, where water is cascading down, filling a spring. There are reeds around the edge and grass fans out around the edges with tall redwood-type trees scattered out of place.

"What is this?" I ask.

"I don't know, but it reminds me of the Lunar falls. Fairies are inhabiting the shores and the trees. Do you see the lights?" He points.

"They've found refuge here. Are we in Terra or New Haven?"

"Good question," Rhydian says, looking around.

A squeak alerts our presence to the fairies, and one flies toward us. The wings move so quickly, like a giant dragonfly, but she is no dragonfly when you properly adjust your vision to her. She hovers in the air at my eye level.

"Is this your new home?" I ask.

She smiles and waves. The pitch of her voice is high and small. I don't completely understand her, but Rhydian says, "We are in Terra, somewhere in the desert. She says this is part of the Lunar Falls, and it's supporting magick here in Terra."

"Is there a way to leave here?" I ask.

Rhydian puts his hand out, and the fairy settles on his hand. Her wings fold behind her back, and her dress shimmers in the light. Her high-pitched voice, without the fluttering of her wings, is easier for me to understand.

"It is but a half day's walk, in the direction you came. However, it is nightfall, and there's no reason to go in that direction. The next town is very far away, and it gets extremely cold at night. It would not be safe to leave the cavern until morning."

My heart skips a beat as Rhydian nods, and I realize we have the entire night together.

"May we stay here?" I ask.

"Of course, my Queen, it would be our honor."

She leads Rhydian and me toward an enormous tree on the other side from where we came from. It's closer to the falls and away from a majority of the fairy lights. When she touches the side of it, a door appears, and Rhydian walks in. The magick is incredible for something so simple. I'm stunned as I walk up the stairs that circle up into the treetop. It's as if I'm in a hotel room from an amusement park. The wood of the tree is smooth. The floors have rugs laid throughout, but it's the open balcony, with lights strung on the rails that come inside along the ceiling where the walls meet. That takes my breath away. A large bed is in the middle with a small stove-like fireplace off in the corner. This must be for someone who stays here often. I turn to the fairy to ask, but she's gone.

"Are you hungry or thirsty?" Rhydian asks me.

On the balcony, I take off my red dirt covered jacket and hang it on the back of a chair. The falls are impressive and mesmerizing.

"No, I'm not hungry. Can you believe this?" I point to the falls and sit in the chair. The water is so blue, suggesting an illumination of light just under it. The open space above, although dark, gives the illusion of stars overhead.

Rhydian sits next to me, his hand close to mine. I'm reminded of when I transported to the beach, having just learned about my father's abduction, and I would need the high council's help. He listened to me and said little. He always supported me.

"Are you thinking about the beach?" He asks.

"I was. How did you know that?"

Rhydian's fingers skim mine on the arm of the chair.

"Just a guess. I don't have access to your thoughts or feelings anymore, but that doesn't mean I don't know you."

The patterns on my arms light up brighter. Is it my magick or emotion?

I stammer, "What do you think we should do next?"

His face turns toward mine. He's so close. "I think

we should get some rest, then make our way out of this cavern and try our best to transport back to your home in Chepstow. It's the safest place, and I'm sure the others are looking for you there."

I agree. I stare up at the darkness, getting denser, as if the sun has completely set somewhere above. Rhydian lays his head back and turns to me. I miss him, and yet he's right in front of me. Why was I so rash in pulling us here and forcing this? I don't regret it because here we are. His eyes are brighter. His lips tilt, making a face that I see in my dreams.

"I'm sorry." We both say at the same time and smile at each other.

He laughs. "For which part? The abduction or almost kicking my ass back there?" His dimple appears first before he continues, "Cross has been training you? I'm guessing from the combo."

I laugh. "Yeah, the drills have become second nature. And I'm only sorry for pulling at the magick of the vow. I'm not sorry we are here and talking. You can't shut me out. It's . . . torture."

His demeanor doesn't change. He leans into me. "Yes, it is, and I'm sorry, Willow. I never meant to cause you pain, ever. Being near you eases my pain, but I needed to feel it; own it. But damn, I missed you."

My breath catches in my throat. "I missed you too."

"Will you forgive me?" His wide, waiting eyes make him look youthful and vulnerable.

"Yes. But I have a condition."

"Really, what's that?"

"Never do that again. You can't just cut me out of your life, Rhydian, and ghost me. That isn't what you do in a relationship unless you want this to be over." I can't bear the thought, and I look away from him toward the ground. "Unless that is what we should do? Is this just too much? That's fine, but you have to tell me."

"Do you want that?"

I shake my head no, and his lips quirk at the side.

"Me neither."

His fingers skim my face, his thumb gliding over my lip. "I miss the connection that the blood vow gave me—the insight of your feelings and thoughts. But my need to know you, protect you, and be with you isn't gone. It wasn't only the blood vow that drew me to you."

The space between us is shrinking.

His lips hover over mine before I connect us. The feather touch ignites a fire in my stomach. One of his hands cradles my neck, the other moving in my hair. Our lips part, and his tongue tangles with mine. I can't get him close enough and what started as gentle feels starved. Somehow, we are off the balcony and on the enormous bed in the room. My hands are pulling at his shirt, his at mine. I need him close to me, and we roll together in an uncoordinated mess of limbs when both our shirts are off, and only my bra remains. My magick hums and pulses in patterns all over my skin.

He kisses designs that appear on my collarbone. I can't help but laugh at the tickle, but before I know it, his lips are back at mine, and he's settled between my legs.

"Willow."

My name a plea on his lips.

His powerful arms are holding him over me.

Be bold is what my brain and body tell me. I don't object when I reach for the waistband of his pants, and he does the same to mine. We don't stop, and it's a blissful connection between our hearts, pain, and experiences. I've never felt passion like this driving me, as if I know exactly what I'm doing versus the bumbling fingers and thoughts before. I'm guided by one purpose: the connection and the intimacy between us together in every way possible.

His hands are skimming over my arms, and he's tasting my shoulder. I kiss his neck—the warmth of his skin transfers to my heat. Blankets are tossed to the floor, and somehow, we are on the floor. I laugh in the tumbled roll, tangled in Rhydian's arms. My hair is a cocoon around us. My naked back tingles when his finger slides up my spine. His other hand tucks hair behind my ear. His face is unreadable with the slight quirk of his lips and his half-mast eyes.

"What are you thinking?" I ask.

"That I'm an idiot, and I wish I didn't walk away as I did. That I don't deserve you."

I don't feel like I deserve him, either. Is that the way of relationships? Each is in awe of the other, not feeling worthy.

"Rhydian, what is deserving anyway?" I hover over his lips. "I know I want you. That's not changed. Is that enough?" I whisper before he leans up to connect our lips.

The kiss is not as urgent as before, but a slow burn that melts my arms and legs into a puddle of wants and demands. I lose track of where we are until Rhydian breaks our kiss. Now my back is on the firm bed.

"Yes. That's a yes, by the way." His breath is fast, his arms strain above me and surround me. "I have to ask, do we?"

I nod and say yes at the same time. We both smile. I've never felt so wanted and beautiful until now. His desire mirrors my own. His eyes never waver from mine. "Are you sure?"

Any uncertain fear is nowhere to be found. I pull him forward so that his body is over mine.

"Absolutely sure."

There is a joy in my half-sleep when I turn and feel Rhydian get out of bed.

"Where are you going?" I mumble, sleep trying its best to overtake me.

"Just adding more wood to the fire and grabbing the blanket for—"

Rhydian sets the blanket on my feet, and a finger skims my lower back. "Wait, Willow, that mark."

Looking over my shoulder, I can't see exactly where he's touching me, but I have all kinds of patterns and marks that are lightly flowing over my body. Laying my head back down on the mattress, I ask, "Is it new? What does it look like?"

"A hex mark."

"A what?" I say into the pillow I'm cradling.

"I've seen it on the dead Wiccans, Demons, other Edayrians. Willow, someone has marked you."

How would I not know I have a hex mark? My shirt is close by, and I pull it on. "What does that mean?"

Rhydian's forehead wrinkles. "I don't know exactly, but we need to get you back to Chepstow under guard, and we need to tell Eoin and the legion council . . ."

His commanding captain side sends tingles low in my stomach. I reach for him and guide him to lie down next to me. The hard lines of his face relax with his shoulders. "Guard? Have you met me?"

"I have, but someone got close enough to mark you, Willow."

He's not wrong. I shiver before Rhydian pulls me in closer to him and pulls the blanket over us. I lay in the crook of his arm and drape my leg over his. The blanket covers us, and my eyes shut.

"I haven't been around anyone that could have marked me. But, Coral, she gave me a note not to trust Emily, Lucy, or Daniel. I know what you're going to say, but they couldn't have—"

He says it anyway. "A valkyrie killed Quinn, Willow. You must know this."

"It's not them. There has to be an explanation." My chest tightens at the thought that either of them would be responsible for Quinn's death, especially Emily.

Rhydian is drawing circles and shapes on my arm.

"It will be fine," he says, but it doesn't sound reassuring when he says it.

I feel my body settle and my mind quiet long enough that I drift into a dreamless, contented slumber with Rhydian's body around mine.

CHAPTER 14

Rhydian is brushing my shoulder with his fingertips. I don't want to open my eyes because when I do, our night together is over. I feel the light on my eyelids and turn my head toward him.

"Willow?"

I nod. "Just a few more minutes—"

His touch is steady and familiar on my shoulder. There is singing coming from outside. Singing that isn't from the fairies because it's loud and clear. Rhydian is rolling out of bed and tugging on a shirt. I try unsuccessfully to be as fluid as he is, but I stumble to the floor, reaching for the rest of my clothes.

Rhydian's half-smirk has me chuckling at myself from embarrassment until I hear the singing more clearly.

"Her name da dada . . . yellow feather in her hair, da da dada dada . . . Cha Cha."

The singing is getting louder. I walk to Rhydian, who is looking out of the knot in the tree on the balcony.

"Is he singing Copacabana?" I ask.

"Um . . . I've never heard that song, but that is definitely Evan."

Evan is turning and smiling, singing, and then he laughs when a few fairies land on him. He begins a new song and goes to the edge of the water.

"Let's talk to him, obviously he knows a way back."

Rhydian nods and follows me. "He's been here before. How does he know of this place? He's speaking to the fairies as if it's something he usually does."

When we exit the tree and walk toward Evan, he doesn't seem shocked at all by our presence. Instead, he waves and sets down a fairy that is in his hand.

"So, you found it! Nice, right?"

Evan smiles, and his eyes sparkle. I wonder if I have a fully lucid Evan. I shake my head because, lucid or not, this is Evan. This is who he is.

"Stumbled upon, actually," Rhydian says.

"Well—I'm not sure about that. Didn't you transport here, Willow? From New Haven's funerals, right?"

I did transport here, but it wasn't something I had aimed for. "Um . . . not purposefully. I didn't know of this place. Maybe you could clear the air on where we are?"

"We are here, of course."

I say nothing but stare at him, and before I ask, he adds, "The Lunar Falls supports the flow of magick. Magick is attracted to magick. Like magnets. It can attract or repel."

I pull my hairband from my wrist and pull my hair into a quick ponytail. "Are you saying it pulled us here? When I transported, I did not have this destination in mind."

Evan touches his nose and winks.

"So how is the Lunar Falls here? Isn't it supporting New Haven?"

"Good, good questions. Yes, and yes. I helped the fairies with the building of this and New Haven. It needed to be split to stabilize the new realm, needed a support structure beyond a pure magickal one. It would help if you had a foundation when you built a house. You need support beams and—"

Evan is droning on about the building of a house and neighborhoods. I'm watching the fairies around him work and do various things at the edge of the water. They are in trees on the other side of the ridge. This massive cave is their home.

"Yes, but where are we?" Rhydian cuts off Evan.

Evan shakes his head and gestures around. "A cavern. Really? Where did you think we were, at a beach or something? I'm doubting his intelligence."

I tug Rhydian back, who is losing his patience with Evan.

"Sorry, but where is this cavern located? Which realm are we in New Haven or Terra?" I ask.

"Did you not hear a word I said? Foundations?" He throws his hands up and puts them on his hips, clearly exasperated with my question, and all I can do is smile because it looks comedic. "Really? Don't you know? Okay, fine. Obviously, wonder boy doesn't, but, Willow, you don't?"

I shrug and reach to hold Rhydian's hand.

"We are in Arizona."

"Arizona? Why would I . . . ?" Oh my gosh, Sabine's house is here in Arizona. "Is this why she's in Arizona?"

Evan smiles. "Do you listen? Again, magick calls to magick. You were pulled here."

"But you did this?" Rhydian gestures around us, and the fairies near us light up. Evan shrugs with a knowing smile.

"Any more questions? Because I'm eager for breakfast with my friends here," Evan says.

I notice the circles under his eyes.

"Yes, I do," Rhydian replies. He gently turns me

around and lifts my shirt to reveal the mark on my back. "Do you know what this means?"

I feel Evan hover near me, inspecting my lower back. His inhale is sharp. "It's a death mark," Evan says flatly. "A hex, the hunters will know you if called."

"How?"

"Detection spells, magick calls to magick. They will use other living things, animals or—"

"Birds," I say before I swallow and look at Rhydian.

"Like a homing beacon," Rhydian replies.

"I'm marked, and the hunters are working to lure me out and do what? Kill me?"

Evan, still behind me, says, "May I?"

I nod before he touches the mark on my back. Looking over my shoulder, his eyes close and the flat of his hand is cool on my back. It's a fast connection before the sweep of my shirt hangs back down. Before I can turn, Evan is in front of me.

"Whoever marked you wants to know where you are and who you are with. I suspect if they wanted you dead, you would have already encountered an assault."

"Do you know what they want?" I ask.

"Eradication of magick, which isn't possible. Therefore, they want to control it or bury it."

Rhydian steps in closer to me, as if protecting me from Evan.

"Why do you say that?" I ask.

Evan continues, "Because not all marks are for death, but they know you, and you know them. Theon and I have seen these marks. I suspect you have too." Rhydian pushes his hand in his hair. "If you use magick, it alerts them. This allows the hunters to find and police you."

"We've got to get to New Haven and tell the Commander. This needs to be reported to the Guardians and Edayrians," Rhydian says.

Evan sits down on the grassy knoll and leans back on his elbows. "He already knows. Several Guardians have this mark, information causes mass chaos, and so the legion council agreed not to share."

"Quinn?" I whisper.

"Actually, no," Evan replies.

Rhydian looks up and says, "Cross."

Evan doesn't deny this, but how would he know? Does Cross know?

"No, this isn't right. Edayrians need to learn what to look out for. We need to talk to the legion council," I say.

Evan checks his watch that doesn't exist on his wrist, and he suddenly stands. We follow him out into the cavern, which is a longer walk than I would have thought. On our way, I ask why we can't transport out, and Evan rambles something about how you don't shake a foundation because that makes a house weak.

When we reach a bend that leads to an opening, the sunlight beckons us toward it.

The sun is bright, and the air is crisp, as if it's still morning. The view outside of the cavern is a desert valley with marbled red and orange in the sunlight. It waves like a river and winds down the mountain we are in. Other mountains are in every direction, and dark green trees and cactus dot the landscape.

"Do you see that ridge, the swirl? That is the closest town. You will need to transport there." Evan says, pointing.

"Wait, we need to see Eoin, the legion council. Remember, you're taking us to New Haven," I reply.

Evan shakes his head and looks at Rhydian. "I have other obligations today."

Rhydian spins on the spot. "How are we getting there? Evan, this is serious. Lives are at stake."

"Lives?" Evan repeats.

"Willow's life, this mark. You must realize it's someone close to her, and those around her are in danger. Guardian lives, magickal lives." Rhydian's tone is even.

"What is it with listening lately?" Evan pauses and looks out at the beautiful landscape in front of us. "They are aware of these marks. This isn't new information. What is new information is your renewed union with my niece?"

My neck and face feel hot. Evan never turns to us

but continues, "Some journeys are starting while others are midway to their destination. It won't take you long to get to Chepstow. The journey is everything, isn't it?"

"Evan—" Before I can protest, he disappears before our eyes.

Rhydian stomps his foot, and the dirt shuffles around his booted foot.

"You may not like it, but there is always a reason. Be patient with him," I say.

"It's dangerous. It's thoughtless. You're his niece, his family, and he seems undisturbed by this mark." Rhydian pushes his hand back through his hair before turning to me. "Don't say it."

"And what is that?"

This should be interesting since he no longer can feel my emotions or the obvious sign that I trust Evan, as crazy as that is. Evan's purpose is always to a larger scale. He embodies the Horned God. Look at what he's accomplished in the cavern behind us. My magick is more controllable, but to accomplish what he has with the fairies, that is something to be in awe of, transporting part of the Lunar Falls to Terra to support magick. Am I doing enough with who I am?

My stomach rumbles loud enough to betray me.

Rhydian's face changes from hard lines to soft ones, with his dimple showing. "Clearly that you're hungry."

I laugh. "Clearly."

He turns me toward the town, reaches for my hands, and interlaces our fingers as he hugs me from behind. The warmth of the sun is nothing compared to the hug and holding of Rhydian. Transporting back to civilization makes our evening and all that's occurred in the last twenty-four hours a part of our past. Does it set the tone for the future? I tamp down the irrational thought.

"Transporting with intention time," I say.

I feel Rhydian hold me closer. When his lips near my ear, he whispers, "You got this."

Facing the small town we will transport to, I focus off to the side of it and take us there in less than a breath.

There is one car that passes us as we walk into the small desert town. Rhydian points to a restaurant in a small strip mall with a large parking lot and grocery store.

"Maybe we should get a quick bite to eat before we go back to Chepstow?" I ask.

"No, we need a plan before we set foot in your home, a neutral ground—the cabin," he says.

"The cabin?"

A few more cars enter the parking lot, and Rhydian pulls me toward him. His face is open, and his eyes wide. "Remember, I took you there from the woods when we first met. Tullen and I went there after . . ." He shakes his head. "Well, after my father died. There isn't food there. Let's grab a few items, and if we can time it right, we can transport there. It's a shorter distance than Chepstow."

It shouldn't matter the distance for us to transport. It's more time alone with Rhydian, so I agree. In the store, we check out our items, and I'm thankful they have electronic pay, so I pay with my cell phone. Rhydian watches a man and woman who are standing and arguing by the automatic doors. When we leave the store, they exit at the same time. Rhydian tugs my hand and leads me to the side of the building. He pulls me behind him around the corner. His finger touches his lips, and I pull my body flush with the side of the building—the brick snags on my shirt.

A full minute passes, and no one rounds the corner. Rhydian turns to me. "Can you tell if there is an opening in the shifting rifts, so we can transport?"

My heart is beating loudly in my ears. I can't hear the pulse. I attempt to slow my breathing and calm myself. The vibration is a low beat, and it's distinguishable, with long and short bursts becoming more frequent. The pause is brief. It's an opening.

Tick-tock.

"Now, we go now." I reach for his hand, but he pulls me into his arms and hugs me.

"Let me guide you," He whispers and lays a kiss on my temple, and his lips stay there right at my hairline. The connection is brief when his magick mingles with mine; I give up the control. We are pushed closer together in the transporting's movement, push and pull, but it's gentle and easy.

Colors of red and brown give way to deep green in the surrounding blur, and our feet settle in our new location. Floorboards groan under our weight. We are on the porch of the cabin. I had only seen the inside of the cabin before.

Lush trees and green surround us. A gravel drive forks around the house and up to the front porch where we are. The air is cool and crisp. Rhydian releases me and opens the front door. Walking over the threshold is a blast to my not-so-recent past. I take in the lazy boy chair Cross sat in, and I can see Tullen and Quinn greeting me in shock. Then Quinn assessing my injury.

Quinn.

How can someone be here then not? This feels different from both Mrs. Scott and my father. I witnessed their deaths. With Quinn, I couldn't bring myself to look at the aftermath of his death.

My thoughts move quickly when I stand in the small space of the living room. I was nervous the first time I was in this cabin—large men all around me, the first time I met Cross, Tullen, and Quinn. Rhydian walks through the small hallway to the kitchen with the grocery bag. I follow him, and he grabs two glasses from the cupboard and fills them with water from the sink, and hands me one.

"Is this your cabin?"

Pulling the glass from his lips, "Yes, it was my grandfather's and has been passed down. My father never particularly liked it, but I would come here in the summers, mostly."

"It's beautiful," I say.

His dimple appears briefly before he says, "It's beautiful and peaceful. No one besides Tullen and Cross would come here. We'll be alone."

My mind wanders, drinking water eases my dry throat.

Why does the word alone have my eyes gravitating down his strong shoulders, back, and the well-rounded butt that his dark jeans curve to? Our night together was . . . He turns, interrupting my thoughts, and hands me a small mixed granola bag and a peeled orange that we bought from the grocery store.

I take them and pop an orange slice into my mouth.

"It's strange to be here, in a unique situation," I say when I swallow most of the orange slice.

"Is it a unique situation? Funny how long ago that seems, but yet, it's not. Everything is so different." His brows draw together, and he's fiddling with the granola bag. "Willow, I—I'm sorry for how I treated you. I don't deserve your forgiveness. You've lost more than I have. Your grief is as fresh as mine, and I punished you for saving us because I didn't know how to—"

I step forward into him, and his hand halts me from hugging him or touching him in any comforting way.

"Wait. I didn't know how to handle my father's betrayal. And not just his betrayal of me, but of everything I stand for and for everything I am. The disappointment in his eyes, his death, they haunt me. I'm still scared of what I could have become had it not been for Abby, my mother leaving, my brothers in arms, for all the small events in my life that pushed me in another way, for your father, and for you even."

"My father?" I ask.

"Yes, Aiden knew my father well enough not to involve my father beyond our introduction. His own words said as much. I don't know why he chose me. He saw my dedication to the Guardians as something that would benefit you. I would have enjoyed knowing him more."

"Rhydian." His name was a whisper of my lips. His eyes finally meet mine.

"Since being near you, the pain that was a consistent reminder of the broken vow has subsided. My head is clear, and I am truly sorry that I didn't realize I was punishing you by being away."

I move again, and this time he meets me, and we hug. The comforting and encompassing kind, with his powerful arms wrapped around my upper back and his head down on my shoulder. He's breathing me in, and I feel a shudder move through him.

"I'm glad we're talking," I say.

"Me too."

"I'm not numb to your pain. I'm sorry for all that you've lost: Quinn, your mother, and your father. Maybe we can comfort each other in the face of it all," I say.

He kisses the side of my face.

"Of all the events that lead us here, I wish what my father orchestrated wasn't one of them, but I would never have traded the blood vow or us willingly. I hope you know that," Rhydian replies.

Placing a hand on his chest, I feel his steady heart. "I do."

His face is a mixture of awe and rawness that I'm not used to seeing. Rhydian is typically self-assured and confident. Right now, in front of me, it's as if he's waiting for a terrible response. Part of me was so hurt and angry when he ghosted me for weeks. That was my selfishness and my need to be comforted after all that happened. He said he needed time, and there was no end date. My timetable was not his. The pain of the broken blood vow a consistent reminder that felt like a rejection, but it wasn't.

"Why, Willow, why me?" His eyes are searching

mine before the quirk of his lips. "Surely it's not all physical, but I can't say I object to that."

I smile and chuckle. "Yeah, I like the physical."

What? Did I say that out loud?

Shaking my head, I continue, "Rhydian, I can't say why, but it wasn't an overnight thing for me. Certainly, there's an attraction, but I respect who you are as a Guardian warrior, your loyalty, your protectiveness, that you treat me as an equal in training and don't mock me for not knowing Edayri but show me and explain it to me . . . I—I fell."

His lips hover over mine. "I fell too."

Our lips connect and test each other before we are open, and tongues tangled. His pull on my waist has our bodies fitted together in such a way that I don't want it to end. Ragged in my breath, I barely register a knock at the door. Rhydian moves so quickly that the sudden coolness of the surrounding air sends me into a moment of vertigo.

"Fuck!" Rhydian says when I hear the door open.

"Now, how's that fer a greeting?" Cross's voice bellows down the hallway.

I wipe my mouth and tidy my clothes, trying to look more put together than I am. In the hallway, I am surprised to see Tullen.

"Hey," I say. I wave awkwardly before putting my hands in my pants pockets.

The squinted eye, assessing me, makes me shake my head at Tullen. His grin says it all.

"The whole, he will talk to me, happened I see," Tullen says. Turning to Rhydian, he continues, "I'm happy to see the reunion, but it's going to be short-lived. We've got a timeline. We have approximately four days before the full collapse. It's expected before the new moon."

"The Commander has requested we escort ya to New Haven. The legion council are meeting in the next day."

I'm still focused on the fact that Edayri is collapsing in four days. If Eoin needs me in New Haven, there must be a reason.

"Why am I needed at the legion council meeting? Did Eoin or Evan say?" I ask.

Cross shakes his head.

"Is everyone out of Edayri?" Rhydian asks.

"Yeah, most who are resettling and grabbing key things. We're ahead of the timeline." Cross pauses before continuing. "It's okay, Willow, I promise. The big issue is these hunters. We don't have a beat on them. They are wide and funded. The hate crimes are not subsiding, so most of Edayri is split between here in Terra and New Haven."

Rubbing the back of my neck, I think about being marked.

"I don't get it. Why mark us and not just kill or attack us on the spot?"

"The theory is that if you're marked, and they have a large group, they look to get the most casualties. It's a follow and scout for a bigger payoff strategy. It isn't well organized. They are clumsy. It's a bonus we found you both here. They ordered Cross and me to scout this area as several High Coven members have property in this area," Tullen says.

Rhydian is leaning on the hall wall. "So, this going to be your home base?"

"Cross thought maybe we could catch you both here."

"A regular Sherlock." Rhydian smiles and pats Cross on the back.

"When do we leave?" Rhydian asks.

After several minutes, we agreed we would leave closer to the evening hours after Tullen and Cross's scouting of the area. Rhydian and I go upstairs to clean up. The upstairs landing has a small hallway with three doors leading to three separate bedrooms. The one at the end of the hall is where Rhydian leaves me.

Out of the shower, looking around the room, I'm comforted being somewhere familiar. The patchwork quilt on the bed in dark maroon and navy colors. The oak chest of drawers. I pull the top draw to find clothes as before—Rhydian's shirts. I run my fingers over them and select a dark one that looks more fitted.

A soft knock at the door before Rhydian peeks his head in.

"Hey, Abby had some clothes here. They have got to be better than my shirts." Rhydian laughs. He's wearing jeans that hang on his hips and no shirt. His wet hair is a ruffled mess. He lays the clothes on the corner of the bed.

Still wrapped in the towel, I hug it a little tighter. "Thanks."

His eyes are watching me and pinched together. "Are you okay?" He stands in front of me and holds my shoulders. "What are you thinking about?"

"Last time I was in this room. I felt insecure and uneasy."

"Why?"

His open eyes are searching mine, and I have a hard time looking at him directly. Are we back to leaving each other? We've both said so much in the last twenty-four hours. I have no idea what it means for the future. Is it stupid that I want to hear the words?

"I guess it's just old memories."

Coward.

"You're not telling me something. After all, we've been through. I thought you were the one who said we needed to talk and not close up."

Great, throwing my own words back at me. The slight sensation in my chest is the squeeze of my insecurities.

"I—I want to know where we stand. We are both going to be pulled into our duties, our jobs, and we've said a lot to each other to mend, but what exactly does that mean?" I ask.

"Willow, is it a label you're looking for? I'm not sure what label I can give us, but I want to be with you. Is that enough for now?"

Gah, I'm silly. I shuffle my feet when his hand gently lifts my face.

"Willow?"

Instead of answering, I kiss him, and he pulls back.

"I want to continue, but with Tullen and Cross waiting . . ."

"Thank you for the clothes. I'll see you downstairs."

Rhydian turns to leave and eases the door shut. I put on the clothes and feel tired. Sitting on Rhydian's bed, I lay down and watch the sun hide behind the blinds one by one by one.

I roll onto my side as he lays a blanket over me.

"It's okay, rest."

I open my eyes, and Rhydian is over me.

"Wait, what time is it?"

"Almost five. You've been asleep for a little over two hours."

Rubbing my eyes, I sit up. "When do you guys want to leave?"

"Tullen came back about twenty-five minutes ago, and we expect Cross in the next half hour."

"What? Have they already looked around? You stayed here?"

He nods before elaborating that he stayed while I slept. They'd report in if they needed backup, but so far, everything is quiet. I follow Rhydian downstairs, and we find Tullen with a book in his lap, head leaned back, and eyes closed.

I'm not the only one who needs rest.

PART III

Enters intention and wishes of the waning moon, brings about the circle of trials.

-The Horned God

CHAPTER 16

Cross's arms are full of fast-food bags and drinks. I open the back door, taking the drinks from him.

"Scouting paid off?" Chuckling, I lead the way into the cabin.

"Actually, it did." He uses his back, bracing the door, so it doesn't slam. However, the thud that sounds makes both of us jump.

"Wha-the?"

Smack.

Two small birds are on the back porch. Rhydian and Tullen come from the front of the house and stand in the yard.

Shit.

"Do they carry the hex identification spell?" Tullen asks.

I reach down over the small dead finch. A light glow lifts from the bird and touches my fingertip. It stings briefly before it evaporates.

"Yes. But the spell is not strong. Someone spelled them a while ago." Shrugging my shoulders, the other small bird struggles to move. "Oh, look, he's okay." I place my hand on the small bird, and the spell evaporates. The bird's head turns in slight movements. It's too tired to fly away. "It's okay. I won't hurt you." I hold out my hand, and it hops in and squats as if it's going to nest.

"You've found a new friend," Tullen says.

"Hmph. Duke, will not stand for it."

Cross's consideration for Duke makes me laugh; it is as if Duke is his dog.

Focused on the woods around the cabin, Rhydian starts toward the porch steps. "We need to secure the area. I don't want to be the next beacon on the—wait a minute."

The guys talk, but my attention is on the tiny bird resting his head on my thumb. I allow magick to warm my hand to keep the bird comfortable. I see the guys are nodding at each other.

"What? What's going on?" I ask.

"Can you redo the magick on the bird? Have it guide us back to where it originated from?"

I look down at the bird. Maybe, but this sweet

little bird trusts me. Heck, he's in my hands. Could I do that? Its eyes are closed.

"I'm not sure I could—What if I hurt the bird? It looks like they both were so tired." I try to keep my voice even. "I mean seriously, look at it in my hands, sleeping! He's traumatized."

Rhydian sits next to me. "Maybe we could go about it differently. You pull the magick back when we reach the destination. Willow, we need to find information about these hunters. It's not safe for any Edayrian here. What happened to Quinn. You are being chased. The magick drew these birds to your mark."

The air is thin at the mention of Quinn's name. With this bird, we could figure out how this originates and possibly stop location spells that help them do these heinous crimes of physical abuse and murder. Maybe there could be a way for us to know who they are. He's right. We should try this.

"How do I do what you're suggesting?" I ask.

Tullen answers, "Call upon your magick to replicate the magickal signature that you touched and place it on this bird. Can you command the bird? Have it show us back to where the magick marked it?"

"You expect me to be Dr. Doolittle here?"

"No, but these hunters are using these birds like carrier pigeons, and we're betting it knows the way home. Otherwise, the signal they give is useless—

unless they are close by and hunting. These spells last longer than a few hours or a day. Why do it any other way? It's strategic. Otherwise, it's a shot in the dark to magick these birds," Rhydian says.

Cross nods. "Makes sense."

"You've seen this before? I don't want to hurt this bird," I ask no one directly, but Tullen responds.

"Something similar to the war games in Guardian training. Willow, it's worth a shot."

I nod. He's right. We have to try. Cross runs into the house and grabs a bag. Rhydian and Tullen are placing spells around the cabin. Me, I'm the babysitter to the little bird in my hands, and I'm thinking about how I'm going to get this little bird to show us where to go so that he can stay right in my hands and continue to rest.

I spy a small bird flying from the west before it falls near Rhydian. Tullen yells from the front of the cabin. Another bird is down.

"I have an idea. Bring them to me," I yell. "Cross, do you have a map?"

"Why?"

"I will pull the magick from the birds, then plot it back into a map. This way, we won't need the bird to guide us. Besides, if someone sees me holding the very birds they are using? The wrong person sees that, and . . ."

Both birds are exhausted but still alive. I pull the

magick spell from both of them and hold it in my hand. The birds' chests rise with what seems like a relief. Cross taps his wrist cuff and displays a map of the United States. He zooms in on the map to where we are.

"Don't zoom in too much. You can do that after," Rhydian says.

The remanent of the hex spells from both birds are in my hands. It's a familiar pattern. This must be the signature. It's the same. It's like a recipe, and the flavors are the same: sugar and vanilla. I push them together, and they easily mix and get stronger. The magick expands and pulses in my hand. It's faint, but I feel its invisible weight. Flexing my fingers, I'm able to move it. I direct my magick to hold the surrounding air, to contain it. Guiding it to the map, the hex magick stays suspended, waiting.

"Here goes nothing."

With my mind, I command the suspended hex and direct it toward its beginning, origin, and home base. It lights up before the hex breaks into threads. The threads fall and dissolve before touching the map, but others land and begin moving into the map.

"It's working," Rhydian says. His eyes are searching the map as the lines settle in. "Zoom out, look." He points toward the east coast. The line goes straight to Massachusetts. Home. "Cross, is this recording?"

"Yes, not my first day."

All the lines settle. It's a beacon where hunters are.

"What did you command exactly?" Tullen asks. His hand under his chin, he isn't looking at the map but at the bird in my hand and me.

"I directed it to its hunter origin."

"Clever. These wonderful little birds just scouted out the hunter's primary operations." Tullen says. "This is amazing. It looks like these hex spells are not original to one location. This reveals everything. Well done."

The guys are all smiles. I can't help but smile as well, along with the satisfaction that these little birds are going to be okay. I've seen too many of them die in my yard in Chepstow.

"Damn, this organization is large: Louisiana, Illinois, Massachusetts, and look at Northern California?" Cross nods to where the lines are the brightest. They are leading into cities.

"Focus, let's see what we can learn here. Then we've got to get this to Commander Eoin. We can ensure the placement is outside of these hotbeds— but see there are locations everywhere. And this is only in the US, whereas this is global, true?"

Tullen nods.

Since I've removed the lingering spells from all three birds, we set them into a gathered towel to hold them while I heal them from fatigue with my touch. They seem to take their time before flying off. The guys are eating while studying the map in the kitchen. Looking at the twilight sky, I wonder if any more birds are flying this way. Rhydian pulls me from my spiraling thoughts.

"Willow. Come in. It's getting chilly out there."

I sit at the kitchen table next to the untouched wrapped sandwich and drink. One chair is open at the table. Quinn is not here. The guys are all business, speaking about strategies that I don't track while I eat. I reminisce about Quinn at this table.

"Look." Tullen points to the map, and near our location in the cabin, a line is pulsing. There are dots on it joining from various directions, like travelers.

"Let's follow it," Cross says.

He grabs the keys, and we all get in the car. I sit in the back with Tullen.

"What do you think it is?" I ask, watching the large pine trees pass as we hit the main road. "Do you think it's a meetup of sorts?"

Tullen nods, but it's Rhydian who says, "I hope so, then maybe we can get more intel to bring to Commander Eoin and the legion council."

"Right, but we're gonna stand out. If they know who the members are—"

"I can magick myself and one of you if I'm able to

touch you safely without the rift, causing chaos in my abilities," I respond.

"Nice." Cross smiles in the rearview mirror. The map projects on the windshield in front of him like a high-tech GPS.

"I don't think we need magick. If we use it, they may have protection or other animals around to warn them. I think we walk in cold," Rhydian says.

"That would put a damper on things." Tullen chuckles under his breath.

Cross takes several turns, and we are coming off the main road and following an old green Ford truck. Another vehicle comes behind us, and it's clear we are in a line of vehicles and are now one dot on the line of the projected map. The back of my neck feels tight. I stretch it from side to side. I want to go with the flow, to go with what this group has planned. But can we only gather intel? After all that has happened? They are killing Edayrian's—anyone with magick.

Show them who you are.

The designs on my hand flare brightly as I close my fist to extinguish my magick.

"I guess we get to join the club," Cross says. He claps his hands and rubs them together when we're halted on the road. "What do you think this big meeting is about?"

Rhydian's eyes were surveying everything. "If I

didn't know better, I think you are ready to knock some heads to find out. Reign that in Cross."

Everyone is sitting upright, muscles tight and ready. We don't know what we're walking into, and regardless of us having magick, it's clear as we pull into an open field and park. They outnumber us. There are over a hundred vehicles here.

"We don't need to start a fight. I thought this was an information-gathering assignment."

Tullen is nodding his head, and Rhydian says in a low voice, "Absolutely, you're right."

The vehicles on both sides of us are empty of people, so we park unnoticed.

"Let's make our big entrance." Cross opens his door, and we all get out of the car and follow.

People gather at the head of the field, where there is an enormous bonfire. Lots of guys are laughing and joking, and I only see a few women. I don't get the impression that this group of people is any different from who I see every day in Chepstow, Massachusetts. Dressed in jeans and coats, nothing reveals they are murderers.

We stay together at the back of the crowd. A speaker comes to life with a tap as someone turns it on.

"Welcome."

A voice booms across the field, and the noise of the crowd quiet.

"As you know, phase three is almost complete."

An eruption of applause begins, and we begrudgingly smile at our neighbors and clap along with them. Except for Cross, he keeps his hands tucked under each armpit. He smirks enough that the biggest guy near him nods, and he bounces back—the hairs on the back of my neck rise. I shift foot to foot, and Rhydian's hand reaches across my shoulder and pulls me into him, and steadies me.

"Willow, it's okay. We are here only to listen," he whispers in my ear.

The booming voice continues over the gathered crowd, "We are lucky tonight that our leader is here. Phase four is underway and will secure our world from being breached by new races who threaten our very existence and way of life." More applause continues. The voice introduces someone, but I don't catch the name.

It's a female voice that takes the mic, "Thank you, thank you all for coming."

I stand on my tippy toes, but I cannot see who is at the front of this crowd. The voice comes across the speaker and apologizes for not being here in person. The voice is commanding and confident. I settle back into Rhydian.

I whisper, "This voice sounds familiar. Are they here or streaming in?"

Rhydian squints his eyes. He taps on Cross and

leans in, and whispers to him. Cross's mouth drops just a little, and he nods his head.

"What? Who is it?"

"I've seen her before. But I'm not sure who she is. She's on a mirrored portal, like a projected screen upfront. Wherever she is, it isn't here. Cross says he's seen her before, too. Thinking maybe someone from Chepstow."

I pull Rhydian's hand and try to guide us through the crowd to see if I can see the speaking woman. Rhydian is right behind me with his hands on my shoulders, nodding to those we are passing. About midway, a behemoth of a guy stands in front of me.

"Where are you going?"

I feel the timbre of his voice in my bones. I shrug my shoulders, trying to maintain my composure.

Rhydian replies, "Sorry, we thought maybe there was some Johnny on the Spot upfront. Girl's gotta pee."

"No one goes upfront without . . ."

"Without what?" I summon the sound of a high-class spoiled brat.

He nods to another guy, and we are being surrounded by men in tight black tee-shirts, which are the security.

"What do I intimidate you?" I shrug and laugh, trying to make light of a daunting situation. I look back at Rhydian, and he nonchalantly shrugs.

The man in front of us smiles. Rhydian turns us, but we are surrounded by large men in dark glasses.

Tick-tock.

This is not good. They probably should intimate me, but they ignited the fire in my blood.

"You don't belong," he says to Rhydian. "You need to leave with her before I get out of hand, brother. And no little girl, you don't intimidate me." His baritone voice is just loud enough that those near us take notice.

We'll see.

"Seriously? Do you enjoy talking down to women? Is it because I'm short, have breasts? Prettier than you are."

Rhydian laughs. Keeping hold of my shoulders, he applies a little pressure. "Dude, we're just pumped and high-spirited. How about you let us pass? She is quite the jungle cat when provoked."

He leans toward us. "I don't think so. I know what you are, and you're not welcome here."

"What exactly are we?" I ask innocently, although inside, my hum is beating under the surface, one taunt, and I'm ready to lay them all out.

"Wiccan."

Okay, we're outed. I'm ready to lay waste to—

"So, doesn't mean we had a choice. You're one too," Rhydian says. I try my hardest to keep my expression even. The guy shows his wrist to Rhydian, and it glows blue with a broken triquetra with thorns on it. My hand is on Rhydian's wrist. I command my magick to imprint the same symbol, and Rhydian shows his wrist and gives the guy a fuck-off look.

"Right. Well, next time, show first, talk shit after." He moves. As we pass, a few of the crowd push their shoulders into us. We get closer to the car. Tullen and Cross are in the car as we open our doors.

"We need to get out of here. Did we get anything useful?" Rhydian asks.

Tullen weekly points toward the front and says, "If you were listening, the plan is complete genocide or subjugation to the Human Principality."

Covering my mouth, I try not to look shocked, and fake a cough.

"The leader's name is Vanessa."

Cross eases the car onto the main road and says, "Did you see when you went upfront?"

"No," Rhydian replies. He explains what happened.

"Did you notice other Wiccans there? What was that Rhydian? How did you know he was, and how did he know we—"

A large truck slams into the car, and we spin.

My head hits the window, and I see blood opposite of me from Tullen.

Rhydian is checking and doing something with Cross.

We are being pushed by another vehicle!

"Grab on to me!" I scream.

Thrusting my hands in the middle of the car, Cross, Rhydian, and Tullen grab my hands. I transport us right out of the car, back to the porch of the cabin, and we land in a jumbled mess of body parts in one pile. Cross groans under me, with Tullen and Rhydian laying over both of us.

"What the fuck?" Cross says.

"Shit, that was brilliant. Thank Goddess," Tullen says as he and Rhydian roll off of me, and I slide off of Cross.

Cross stands quickly.

"They will follow that signature. We have to go," Rhydian says. He touches my temple. My blood is on his finger.

"Okay, one more time, fellas? I'm on a roll." I hold out my hands, and they each hold on to me. I transport us smoothly between the pulse and a shift of the rifts, straight to New Haven. Because there is no way I'm leading those assholes back to Chepstow.

CHAPTER 17

The stairs to the Hallowed Hall are the same in New Haven as they are in Edayri. I do a double-take because this is New Haven, right? I'm familiar with all the surrounding structures. At the mass funeral gathering, I didn't see this many structures and buildings. It's the same, but feels different. Edayri has a particular flow about it, a peace that I felt. When I first came to Edayri, it was the connection; it could've been from my magick or my family's heritage, but here, it's like a sterile surgical room, practical but not somewhere you live.

Evan is standing near us, looking at his fingernails as if he's bored and we are late. Did he realize what would occur from that cave to here for me and Rhydian?

"We need to speak to the Commander and Sabine," Rhydian says.

Evan points behind him. The flowing cape of Sabine is heading in our direction, and Commander Eoin is fast on her heels.

"Willow! Oh, my Goddess. Are you okay? What are you doing here?"

Her questions continue as she looks me over.

Evan interrupts, "Willow has a situation, and it was important for me to get her to safety along with the captain of the Guardians."

"Evan—"

He taps his temple. Did he see that we'd end up here? If he's so omniscient, why doesn't he stop all of this?

Commander Eoin moves in front of Sabine and invades Evan's space. His stubble is almost a full beard, which is at odds with a usual clean face. The dark shadows under his eyes. His stoic nature heightened by the deaths of so many, including Quinn . . . someone he loved.

"What do you mean? And you thought it was safer to bring her here? Cross and Tullen are in Chepstow. Didn't you think it might be wiser to take her to her home?"

Cross and Tullen step to the side, and Eoin sees them and clamps his mouth down.

"Commander. Sabine. The hunters—we infiltrated

a meeting, gained a mapping of their locations. They call themselves the Human Principality. Their goal is genocide of magickal peoples or to subjugate them for their use," Tullen reports to Eoin.

"How so?" Sabine asks.

"Magickal beings are helping them. Wiccans even," Rhydian says.

"Possibly valkyries as yer aware." Cross's voice isn't the booming sound it usually is. Eoin's face is stone. Cross looks away before he continues, "We recorded what we could on my wrist band for you, sir. We spread out so we could gather as much intel as we could."

Eoin nods. "That's good. Debrief now. Let's catch up with the rest of the teams."

I watch the four of them jog up the stairs and disappear between buildings.

The tension is steady in my neck from the scrutinizing stare down by Sabine. I breathe deeply because people are watching us. If she's taught me nothing else, it's maintaining my composure in front of a crowd.

"Should we talk here or in private? Because I realize you are hiding things from me. Let me tell you what I'm aware of now. This Human Principality group is marking us, using us, and ending us. And how do I know this?"

Sabine is looking at Evan because she knows.

He gestures to my back as I pull up my shirt at my waist to reveal the mark to Sabine.

"I'm marked. I don't know by whom, and the intention isn't clear. But you learned about hex marks, and I find out by happenstance this is . . . how would you say? Unacceptable." I grit the last word between my teeth.

Her face drops with a slight shake of her head.

"Somewhere private, now. Follow me," she says.

I follow behind her bellowing purple cloak as she leads the way from the grand entrance of the New Hallowed Hall. We pass by the pillars that stand high as if they have been here for centuries, but they have only recently transferred them here per Sabine talking as we walk. It is amazing what the legion council has accomplished.

Sabine turns a corner behind a large building that is being used as a judicial forum and crosses to a smaller one. She opens the door with a flick of her wrist, and we enter a smaller room that leads into a larger hall. The marble floor clicks under her shoes as we move into a room and find several people at tables with laptop computers and headsets on.

"We need the room," Sabine announces. Those sitting stand up quickly, as if eager to leave for a break. Abigail, Rhydian's sister, comes from the back of the room. I wonder if she knows I was with her brother this whole time. Thaxam comes in from a side door. We sit at a small table, except for Evan, who seems halfway between sitting and standing. He leans on the table.

"What is going on?" Abigail asks no one in particular when Sabine responds.

"Hunters have hex marked Willow. They are larger and more coordinated than we've guessed at. They call themselves—what did you say, the Human Principality?"

Evan adds, "But it's clear this group has magickal beings helping them, Wiccans and valkyrie that we are aware of."

"Your friends may not be your friends. They killed Quinn in a way a valkyrie would, with a lightning strike," Ax says. His voice leaves no emotion. He's laying down the facts. I hate Sabine, nodding her head in agreement.

"This isn't Emily or Daniel."

Evan looks away as if listening to someone. "But . . . you're not sure."

He's right. I understand how it looks. I would point to them if I didn't know them. Heck, Daniel has had all the opportunities living in the same house as me.

Do you know who they are?

"Cross is marked as well," Evan says, his eyes unmoving.

"He is?" Abby responds.

Ax answers, "He doesn't realize he's marked? I suspect you didn't either, Willow. That is until it revealed itself and someone saw it."

I look at Ax and Sabine. My voice changes, more profound and dripping with disappointment. "Are you telling me you won't tell Cross, but you suspected he is marked? Please tell me that isn't true."

"He knows," Evan says. "Quinn pushed Cross out of the way. Quinn wasn't a target, only a bystander."

If my mouth drop doesn't show my frustration, then it would be my wide eyes. "Evan, if you see all of this, why aren't you stopping it? Could you have—"

"No. Some events I don't see until they decide. Pieces of a puzzle. The complexity of the whole."

I stand and turn on him.

"You should have done something! Said something!" I yell.

He doesn't respond. Evan only stares with eyes that are knowing and sad. I want to scream more, but I can't because I understand what it's like when you can't do anything but watch something happen. He couldn't have done anything. It would have been too late. I imagine what he has interfered with to have a better outcome.

Yes, Willow. I'm regretful for your continued grief.

The sting of his words in my head allows a tear to fall before I wipe it away.

Willow, accept completely who you are. This is not one-sided.

"I don't understand," I reply aloud.

It's Ax who answers. "Soldiers die. It doesn't matter, mark or no mark. These hunters, or whatever they call themselves—The Human Principality. We are at war, there and here."

Talking to Evan about his comment privately to me will have to wait.

"So, those marked are not limited to Terra?" I ask.

"No. I've seen several in New Haven. It's not safe anywhere," Ax responds. "We suspected, but our kind is joining their cause. We could have spies here."

"Why would anyone do that?"

Abby responds, "Easy. Anyone who thinks that their life is better without rule and a caste system. Someone could easily sway them. This world is collapsing. If they think they can save themselves or their family in Terra by giving up magick, an option to blend in equally? Willow, it is not so far-fetched. We've only just begun with the legion council. I'm sure many doubt it's staying power."

"This is true. They designed the crown for fear and order. You've changed that. But you, Evan, our family is powerful, and that is a threat to anyone if the old ways return," Sabine says.

Why is this so complicated? I gave up the royal power. I'm just a figurehead in disagreements. I form the legion council of all beings, not just Wiccans or High Covens. Clutching my hands, my nails dig into my palms.

"Why do you need Evan and me? If we go in guns a blazing, doesn't that push us backward? The old ways?"

Evan is pacing on his side of the table. Is it so much to ask him to sit? Goddess, he is always on the move.

"They need us to use our magick, our combined power," he says.

I want to help, I do, but I feel like a toy forced to play a part.

No, you're the embodiment of a goddess whose people are asking for your help. You are the Crown, the Queen of Wiccans. Covens are not coming of their own free will to the aid of Edayrians.

Evan, I pissed off the covens. I made the hierarchy useless.

True.

"Care to share with the class?" Abby asks.

I shake my head and see they are all watching me and Evan, waiting.

"Let's go have a chat with the legion council. I presume they are waiting for us?" Evan asks.

Abby leads the way. They are in the same main building that's part of the Hallowed Hall. Evan holds the door open to the grand circular room. I remember meeting the high council in this room. That seems so long ago. Me asking for help and later learning one of the high council members was one who tortured my father—all a plan to get to me, to manage and control the Wiccan crown.

It's the same large circular table that sits in the middle of the massive room. The difference now is that there are many chairs around it instead of five key chairs at various points. Aren is the first to welcome us. She's closer to my age and seems out of place within the high council. She's a powerful Wiccan, and someone I think I could be friends with. We share similar ideals. Little did she know that when she joined the legion council in its inaugural year, they would elect her the chairperson. I remember the day she stood up to join against her mother's will, pulling at her arm to stay seated.

Aren sighs. "I suppose we should get right to it. But I'd like to wait for—"

A man with long hair and pointed ears walks in, waves, and sits down at the only empty seat.

"Well, we are all here then."

Aren's has come a long way from looking at her nails in boredom, as she was the first time, I met her.

It feels as if Evan and I are tourists. Everyone is looking at each other in greeting, except Evan. When I look at him, he's staring straight up at the ceiling.

"Pst. Evan, what are you doing?" I whisper to him

from the side of my mouth. I mean, Evan does strange things that I should be used to, but I can't help wondering.

Not moving his head or his eyes, he responds to me with the side of his mouth, "Getting the feeling of the room. Everyone's quite nervous. This should be interesting." He closes his eyes before looking straight ahead at Aren. Although she's on the other side of the table, the acoustics must've carried Evan's comment.

"You're quite right. Let's get on with it," she replies. She looks at the other members, and everyone nods in agreement. "As you're aware, we want to reinstate temporary royal intervention in our transition and refuge efforts. We have tried democratic methods, but the most powerful among us in the noble covens won't help because the hunters are targeting them, so they refuse to use magick for others."

Evan smiles, and his fangs are prominent when he leans into the table and puts his hands on the edge. "So, what are you thinking? Prayers to the Goddess and Horned God have delivered us here as saviors? Or —do you want penance because you blame us?"

I suck in the air too sharply.

"We didn't start the Convergence. Mr. Boward started all of this for power and control," I reply. My voice is gruffer and louder than I had intended.

Ax is the first to respond, "You haven't seen the numbers, Evan. Hundreds have lost their lives, and every day the murder tally rises. The Guardians are not enough, and without help, we will dwindle. But you already understand this, or else you wouldn't have helped the fairies and others."

Evan sits back, looking relaxed. I sit stiffly and clench my hands together. Ax said hundreds have died. All I see is my loss, and then everyone else passing with them. The people that anchor me to a home are gone, and those that are helping me rebuild a family are in jeopardy. The little girl that lost her family the night Quinn lost his life. Her future is forever changed, not unlike mine when my mother lost her life saving me. No more children should lose their parents like this.

"I'll help. What do you need?" I say.

Aren and Ax both smile weakly at me. Maybe it's not me they want, but damn it, it's me they will get. Their eyes shift to Evan.

"That was not the response I thought I would get."

Evan puts his hand on my shoulder. "Actually, they need us both. One will not complete the needs required, so if I say no . . ."

"Sorry, so how do we help?"

"Communications on a wide scale. We need to move Edayrians to the refugee camps, both in New Haven and in Terra realms. We need reinforcements of check-ins and reports, so that we can mobilize Guardians effectively."

I nod to Ax. "Okay, how do we do this?"

"We have a system set up for communications, and we have talking points for you both," Abby replies.

Evan and I agree. We complete our recorded messages into what looks like an older phone.

Ax explains that it's an old magick that connected Edayrians and all inhabitants to the Wiccan crown when new laws were decreed, or announcements were made. It feels wrong to me. I can't imagine receiving a communication in my head this way from someone. I hope this really helps. The legion council members leave the grand room.

"Well done." Sabine hugs me.

"I hope that Wiccans and Edayrians heed the call to help where needed and stop hiding in the shadows. But with these rifts from the Convergence, it isn't safe, regardless. I can't blame anyone for wanting to protect themselves and their family."

His deep voice startles me more than his red skin, enormous body, and massive horns. "And this makes you different from your predecessors. This crown and power do not consume you to rule and subjugate. You understand this and your actions show this."

I hug him and catch him off guard. "Thank you. I hope all see it this way. I don't want to repeat the past."

The man with pointed ears stops before leaving the room, giving an odd smirk to Ax.

Sabine's smile reassures me while Evan is still pacing. Abby has left us to talk with the legion council members.

"It's a new era, there is no repeating the past at this point." Ax responds as I let go. I see his fangs in an awkward grin. "Usually Wiccans are intimated by me, not hugging me like a teddy bear."

Laughing, I respond, "Sorry, they don't appreciate what they're missing then."

"Right—I think I prefer intimidation; otherwise, my fellow demons will think I've gone soft." His laugh shakes the seriousness out of the room, along with the weight of all that is coming.

CHAPTER 18

Evan and I marvel at how nothing looks different here in New Haven. He's walking toward the Goddess Fountain down the steps toward the garden. How they have moved everything from one realm to this new one is beyond my comprehension. We near the edge of the fountain. I see a ripple in the air like you do on a hot summer day, but here it's like a crisp fall day. Rubbing my eyes doesn't help because I see it again, over the water of the fountain.

"I feel it, but you see it?"

"What exactly am I seeing, Evan?"

"Something is off here, in New Haven. Besides the fact it parallels Edayri, it's . . ."

"It's like a haunted shell," I say.

"Exactly. Where is the grounding magick of this realm?"

Looking around, I realize no one is around us. The next ripple in my vision is over the water again, and I point it out to Evan. My magick hums to life and rises to my skin. I'm pulled forward and stumble over the edge of the fountain into the water. Evan doesn't hesitate. He steps into the water with me. Shoes and all, it submerges us up to our calves.

I'm not sure why I feel so bold, but I reach out before it goes away, and my fingertips look like they have disappeared. Then, of course, I sense them, but it's as if my fingers are in a different place than my body.

"Evan, this is—" I watch him walk right into the ripple in front of me and disappear.

My hand in midair, I follow him and run right into his back in the same spot we just were, but not. It's the Goddess Fountain, but different. I turn, and the ripple moves elsewhere. The steps of the Hallowed Hall are empty, and the buildings missing.

"What is this?" I ask. I follow Evan over the edge of the fountain ledge. Sloshing with my wet shoes and pants.

He spins in a circle.

"This is New Haven—where we were, is not."

"How do you know that?"

"Magick attracts magick." He nods toward gardens. Although it's empty here, it's lush and colorful.

The sun is warm on my face. I breathe in the fresh air. It fills my lungs and radiates down to my toes, filling me and grounding me. Magick flows on my arms and hands. Evan is correct. This is where magick has taken hold. Being quiet and truly listening, it's ringing in my body. The hum is a soft tone in my ear, a beautiful melody. Magick.

"Why are we the only ones—"

Evan turns, and his horns catch the rays of sun and gleam, his eyes bright and large. "Because we are tied to the creation. They are not."

"How are we tied to creation?"

"The OGs are moving on, Willow. When the Goddess crowned you, she chose. You only need to tap in and truly accept it."

Some of the crazy that comes out of Evan's mouth. That can't be right. I've accepted who I am. I've been through hell and back, and I'm the freaking Wiccan Queen. I've dived in with both feet!

His eyebrow arches.

"What! Spit it out." I raise my voice.

"No."

"Is this for real?"

"How can there be a Horned God without a Goddess?" he asks me, as if I know the answer.

"I don't know, shouldn't you know? Aren't you what the embodiment of the Horned God?"

That same arched eyebrow pops up again.

Do I deny myself? Wait a minute. "Aren't the Goddess and Horned God-like lovers? Come on, that is—" I can't finish my sentence and regress to pointing between us.

But Evan laughs so hard he bends from the waist.

I can't help but laugh at him. "Gross, right?"

"Besides the fact we are family, and I'm like too old for you, yes. Absolutely yes!" His laugher dies down as he wipes a tear away. "How can you call me the embodiment without stating that of yourself?"

"Well, I don't feel any different. My magick is the same—but, oh."

There are differences. Magick, it's always been strong since being unbound, but when the Goddess crowned me directly. When she did that, I was tested in trials. It comes back to me, all the versions of her placed on me. The clothes, the hair, all in rapid succession. I only thought she was testing me as the Wiccan Queen, not a test as her successor—I clearly don't pay attention. I'm an idiot.

"Clearly," Evan replies. "Do you really think the power of how easily controlling magick comes from the crown and your family legacy?"

My mouth feels dry. I swallow, wanting to respond, but don't.

He is observing the gardens and walks away from me. I do the opposite and follow the hum internally.

The flow of the grounding nature I feel. I am strong and connected, as I was with the fairies in the cavern.

The Lunar Falls is here like it is in Terra. This is confusing. Because if magick is here, and this is New Haven, then we were in Edayri . . . but everyone believes it's New Haven.

"Oh, my Goddess. Evan, this is a set-up," I stammer.

"It's genocide, Willow. It's an efficient way of killing, and the Human Principality is responsible."

This confirms the fear from Ax. It would mean they have someone on the inside in Edayri. Someone with magick who is doing this here.

"Yes." Evan breathes as if listening to my thoughts. "We must course-correct, otherwise . . ."

"Can we trust it isn't someone on the legion council?"

"We won't know until we see opposition. Those who deceive are crafty."

"So, you believe it's someone on the legion council, now?"

Evan smiles. "Don't put words in my mouth. I didn't say that. You did. Maybe your intuition is something you should listen to more often. The Goddess side of who you are—your empathic, listen to yourself more."

I see the ripple over the water again. The mirror

of what New Haven should be is mocking us. It's Edayri, a doomed place with people walking and moving throughout it. They are unknowing, and the thought of everyone on that side dying is too much to comprehend.

"Can we reverse this?"

"Edayri is a mirror. This is a brilliant madman, actually. A fake that you're building—a safe realm in one spot—only to realize it's the same quicksand you were trying to escape. Lastly, you pick off those on Terra. Everyone is fearful. You achieve all that you want."

"I think it's a madwoman."

"You're right; we have to reverse this."

"Wha—How, Evan?"

"We roll up our sleeves and get to work."

Tick-tock. Tick-tock.

Okay, now I feel the frustration Rhydian usually feels around Evan.

"Everything precious to me, beside you, is on the other side of that mirror is a collapsing realm! I need more than we roll up our fucking sleeves, Evan! Tell me specifics. Do you know a spell?"

His face is one of amusement, and the heat of my face only becomes more intense.

"I swear to the Goddess! If you—"

"Yourself, Willow. You swear on yourself?"

"What?" I say, exasperated. "What do you mean by that? She is still very present. I don't understand your riddles and comments on the embodiment." My frustration is mounting out of my mouth. The words spill without thought. "Just tell me what to do. How to do it. If you're all-powerful and embody the Horned God, why wouldn't you want me to do the same? Save everyone we can? I don't think I can handle more death and destruction. That's all this stupid crown is, it's death!"

"Willow, stop embodying the Goddess—you have to become her, or better yet, become the full you, isn't that all she asked?"

He's insane. I met the Goddess. She blessed me. Nothing more, just as the Horned God did to Evan. Right?

"What did you do then?" I ask, sarcasm dripping from my lips.

"I became the full me and embraced it, accepted it. You may think a god lives forever, and I suppose they can in some form or another. But, own it and believe it, shed the idea you know nothing because you, in fact, are a creator and a protector of your people. You prove this time and time again, yet never believe it."

"Sometimes it is easier to believe what you know."

"That's crap, and you know it. Don't be lazy."

Evan's face is hard now. His stare has me step away from him. "You don't want to see what's in front of you: your power, your potential. The truth about your friends. You're afraid of conflict, but what's worse is you won't join the fight for yourself. Where is that girl?"

"I lost most of my family, Evan! Sorry, I want to keep those around me the same. I hate to think that my friends would . . ."

"Betray you? Use you? You're smarter than this. What you need to learn the hard way every time?"

"Evan." I shake my head. I see Rhydian, Sabine, Cross, and Tullen gathering at the stairs of the Hallowed Hall on the other side of this mirror gate. They look concerned and are calling my and Evan's name. They can't see us.

"They are looking for us," he says before he walks through the gate. I follow him, and as I step through, I'm being pulled back.

"Evan!" I scream, reaching out. It's Rhydian's hand that grabs mine, and then Cross that grabs the other hand. They are pulling.

"Fuck, what's this?" Cross yells.

"The hard way," Evan says before he pushes the three of us back with magick, and the gate closes. We are flying and being pushed and pulled. The wind is strong.

"We're being transported," Rhydian yells, clamping onto my wrist with both hands.

I can barely open my eyes. We are spinning too fast.

"Where?" I yell.

"Don't let go," Cross says as we all land flat on our stomachs on green grass with a hard impact.

CHAPTER 19

Tick-tock, tick-tock.

I roll onto my back and stare up at the dark, clear sky.

"Rhy?" Cross groans.

"Still here."

The lush grass hugs me and evades my nose. I roll over and see them pushing themselves up from the ground.

"The hard way? Damn, your uncle is just—" Rhydian helps me up.

The moon and stars are bright. It's easy to see where we are.

"Well, what do ya know," Cross says. He points at my father's house. We've transported to Chepstow.

I'm staring at the back of the house with three,

no, four people on the patio. A car is driving down the driveway.

Pointing at the car. "Stay down."

Crouching down, we tuck into a shadow from the tree line at the edge of the property.

There is someone or something near to us in the tree line. We are not alone. They are arguing. Rhydian points and moves behind a tree trunk further into the grouping. And that's when I realize who it is: it's Lucy. The tenor of a muffled response signifies Daniel is with her. Why are they hiding?

Who is on the patio? I squint and realize it's Marco with others I don't recognize.

He's going back into the house when those he was speaking with transport. Maybe they are Guardians, or is it the Human Principality?

The car is pulling up toward the front of the house is Coral's car. Maybe she's looking for Lucy?

Rhydian is giving Cross directions without speaking using hand signals. He points at the opposite edge of the property. I point to the front of the house, and he nods.

Coral is knocking on the front door. I transport when Marco answers the door. My heart is skipping with the clock in my head, and I transport right into the foyer. Coral's hand is shaking. She hands a note to Marco. He slowly opens the note.

"Ah!" Coral screams.

Marco doesn't miss a beat, despite my sudden appearance.

"What's with this note, Coral?" Marco asks, handing it to me.

She shakes her head fast. "You read it, so you know. I can't—I can't say . . ."

There is a wavering dark iridescent thread with thorns around her. She has magick holding her. I see it now and sense the spell. How is that possible? Instead of doubting, I close my eyes briefly, and it's as if I can still see the threads binding her threatening to hurt her. Someone powerful has placed this on her.

"They bound you," I say.

She nods her head.

"The spell would alert someone."

Coral's eyes are pleading and confirming.

And I realize that she's taking significant steps to avoid something.

"And you can't answer for fear of breaking that spell. So, tell me, what are Daniel and Lucy doing here hiding in the tree line? Do you know about the dead birds in my yard?"

Marco's eyes don't give away any surprise at my statement. He only responds to seeing Cross walk in from the back of the house.

Cross nods to me, "All clear."

Coral's eyes are welling with tears. When she wipes her cheek, I see the band-aids on her fingers.

Examining the note's ink, it's clear that this is not standard ink. It's Coral's blood. Someone has prevented her from speaking and using ink to communicate. Blood to paper was her only way, and she did this. She pained herself to warn me not once, but twice.

"I can protect you. What is going on with Lucy? Is Daniel involved?"

"Shit." Marco says.

"I can't. My father—" She yelps and bends forward. I'm at her side, and Cross is carefully watching while listening to Rhydian over the ear comm.

"She's cursed. It's a signal beacon, Willow." Cross says deadpan. "It's not holding—whatever is keeping her quiet." Addressing Coral, he presses her for information, "You might as well let it go because Rhydian just overheard the interlopers tell someone ya finally broke."

It was enough to push Coral to the floor in a blubbering heap.

"Coral!" Marco drops to her.

"She's gonna kill him. I know she will."

Cross and I are in front of her. Cross asks, "Kill who?"

"Her father," I respond before she can.

Cross pins Marco with a stare. "You don't know

any of this? Who was on the patio a few minutes ago?"

"Guardians looking for you all. What's going on?" Marco looks genuinely confused. "Why do you think Daniel would have anything to do with this?"

"She's coming for you and your kind, Willow. You, Marco, anyone with magick and who's different. But, Willow, she knows what and who you are. Because of Lucy and Daniel."

I tense at their names. Inside, my heart wants to know why, but my head doesn't care.

"Fuckin' hell. Who? Who is coming?" Cross says, helping Coral up in one smooth step.

"My father's wife, my stepmother Vanessa." Coral takes a shallow breath.

Vanessa. I feel the tingle up my back. The black smoke, the whip, the broken triquetra with thorns. Graduation. It all clicks.

"She is the leader of the Human Principality," I say.

Coral's hands shake, and I hold them. My hum illuminates across my skin. Then, with little thought or direction, I pull the wavering thread surrounding Coral and snap it. Her exhale is one of relief. The curse that caused her pain is no more, but it will also confirm to her jailor that she is no longer controlled.

"We need to leave to keep you safe."

"But where? I can't leave—"

I turn to Cross.

"Sabine's new place?" Cross offers.

He's right. That would be the best opportunity, and she can help Coral there. Maybe retrieve her father?

The ticking of the clock continues. The metronome beat is present in my chest. This is a countdown, and it's getting too close.

"I've not been to Sabine's. How can I transport there, and what about the rifts? Can you tell if it's good? Otherwise, we could end up anywhere," Cross says.

"Coordinates. Meet us there. I'm taking her."

I swirl my hand, and the numbers flicker in the light's glow. "Scan them, save them so you can meet me there."

Cross taps on his wrist cuff and does exactly as I ask him, and now he can share Sabine's location to Rhydian and transport there.

"I can't leave. Willow—she has powers, she—poisons and controls. She can—" Coral is shaking.

"So do I. I'm powerful and I don't think you forgot that small tidbit. You wanted my help, Coral. So let me help."

I grab her wrist and tug her through the front door and transport us.

Daniel is calling out to me, but the sound fades as we do.

CHAPTER 20

We arrive at Sabine's house. Coral pulls her wrist from me and starts yelling. This causes Sabine and several members of the household to come running into the foyer.

"Willow? Who is this?" Sabine asks.

"I'll tell you who I am. I'm the friend you just kidnapped, Willow! You have condemned my father and me. She's going to kill us both. What have you done!"

"She will not kill you or your father. Let me do what I need to and protect you both."

The tears that were streaming down Coral's face take a reprieve. She spins and looks at everyone around her.

"Who are you people?"

"Why can't I trust Lucy and Daniel? Is Emily involved? You trusted Marco. He's not involved?"

Her shoulders are bobbing with her sobs. "They have a different magick, and they are using it to tag and hurt people. Willow, they are helping her. They knew of the curse on me. Lucy is the worst and does it all without control. Emily is compliant, which is just as bad. Marco knows nothing but is getting very suspicious of Daniel and Emily."

Sabine touches Coral on the shoulder and says to her, "It's okay, sweetheart, you are safe, and I'm going to go get your father and bring him here." Coral seems settled by Sabine's calm words. Sabine touches Coral's forehead, holds her back, and finally her shoulders relax down, and her eyes blink slowly.

"Yara, can you kindly take Coral to one of the guest rooms on the east side?"

As Yara leads Coral away, Sabine turns to me.

"She warned us her stepmother, Vanessa, is the head of the Human Principality, the hunters. She placed a curse on Coral so that she could not speak about any of it. So, apparently, she has powers. I think my friends are being influenced by magick or, if Coral is right, working with Vanessa."

"Well, first thing is first. You're safe here. There are plenty of enchantments around this home on the side of the mountain. Of course, no one knows of this place, but I need Tullen." She calls for him, and he walks into the room.

"We need to go get Coral's father now. You must stay here, Willow. Tullen?"

Tullen mutters into his ear com and then says, "Let's go. I have the coordinates and address."

"Willow, it's going to be important to get Evan involved. Based on what he's told me about the mirror gate, you both need to be together to break or flip the gate from the old Edayri to New Haven. I'll be back as soon as I can."

Everything is going so quickly.

Sabine and Tullen transport before I can think of asking a question. I'm left alone, looking around at this massive house. The tile floors, the stucco walls, it's so very different from Chepstow.

Evan. If you can hear me, I'm in the thick of it now.

I hear the paws of Duke on the tile coming toward me. I squat down, and he comes to me, and I hold on to him as he sits. Thankfully, he's here and Sabine's moved almost everything here.

"Be a good boy. I'll try to come back in one piece."

He licks the side of my face.

Tick-tock, tick-tock.

The wind shifts around me as if air conditioning turned on overhead. As soon as it stops, I look up to find Evan standing over me.

"So, this is the new MacKinnon Manor?"

I shrug. "Yeah, I guess so."

Evan walks around, peeking down the hall. "Well, I gotta say I like this better than the gloom and doom of tradition in the highlands of Edayri."

He's not wrong. The wood is lighter, the paint here is pale, nothing is dark, everything is terra cotta and light.

I stand, and Duke runs down the hall as if he heard food.

"So, it's all coming together?" He asks.

Sometimes I just don't understand his comments. I shake my head.

"Coming together? Are you serious? Evan, this is a disaster. My friend's involvement, and there's a mirror gate, and what they planned is horrific. Eradication of innocents, just because they were born different or have magick?"

I feel the air shifting within the house. Cross, Rhydian, and Commander Eoin all appear.

I open my mouth, but Evan is already speaking before I can muster the words to say anything.

"When the Convergence finishes, it will collapse on Edayri and all those who are in it. The HP has put a mirror gate that makes it look like everyone is safe. Little do they know they are in Edayri, not New Haven. That's where she's coming up with the eradication comment."

Boy, does Evan know how to get to the point.

Commander Eoin's face doesn't budge. Maybe he was aware of it or had an inkling before now?

"How much time Evan? How much time do we have?" he asks.

"I don't think we have a lot of time. Willow, you hear it and feel it now, the pulsing, it's getting closer together. It's soon, an hour, maybe more?"

"What? An Hour?" Rhydian asks.

"Evan, I know who the leader is of the Human Principality. Her stepdaughter is down the hall. Whatever plans she had, she'll move them up. But, unfortunately, the element of surprise is no longer on her side. When Sabine and Tullen return with her father, maybe they will know more, but I suspect Vanessa will be prepared."

Cross interrupts, "Wait, she doesn't know that ya all know of the mirror gate they have put in place. I don't think Coral knows anything about that."

"Maybe we should talk to Coral and find out? I could talk to her," Rhydian says.

I'm sure Coral would enjoy that. Can't believe that thought of jealousy entered my mind. I'm an idiot. Because it's Rhydian. Maybe that would put her at ease. However, she came to me to warn me.

"I think it's best if I talk to her. However, right now, she's taking a nap—courtesy of Sabine."

Yara comes in from the back hallway with Theon.

"I have another looking after our guest. Sabine will

come shortly, and I have several of the house staff who will help you move as many as we can to New Haven or here to Terra."

Evan smiles broadly and opens his arms as if he's going to hug everyone. "Nothing brings people together like a disaster."

Theon winces and shakes his head. Rhydian's waiting face smirks as he rolls his eyes at Evan's response.

"Yes, as Commander, I take the help gratefully. Evan, you and Rhydian stay here with Willow. Cross, Theon, and I, along with Yara and other members, will go to New Haven. Rhydian, reach out to Abby and Ax, let them know we need emergency counsel help." Eoin looks down at his cuff that has timing of the rifts. "Tell them we'll be there in less than five minutes at the center of the Hallowed Hall near the fountain."

"What do you need me to do?" I ask, waiting for some direction.

"Wait for Sabine to return—" At the drop of my face, Eoin continues, "Then go confront your friends in Chepstow. We no longer are going to wait for them to bring chaos to us. Stop it there, then join us in New Haven. We need all the help we can get."

Evan slaps his hands together and rubs them maniacally. Rhydian's face is almost comedic. I can't help but bust a huff of a laugh.

"What, you just want me to show up in front of Lucy and Emily and say: what the fuck?"

"Exactly! Confront your so-called friends. Because if I do, knowing they carry responsibility for the death of Qu—" His voice drifts on Quinn's name. "I won't waver. You shouldn't either. They have no respect for you." Eoin looks away from me and turns.

My heart thumps, and the breath gets stuck in my chest.

"Will do, Commander," Rhydian responds.

I feel the change in the house when Sabine transports in with Mr. Lee. He is passed out, leaning on Tullen's shoulder. Theon and Yara help Tullen, and they add Mr. Lee to the same room with Coral. Sabine explains he was resistant to coming with her, so she had to improvise.

"His wife, Vanessa, has riddled their home with enchantments and spells that are quite difficult to get around. I know she'll be aware, if not already, that both of them are gone. I had to pull some of her magick off of him. She is a powerful Wiccan. It was easy to recognize her magick signature. Why she wants to end magick isn't clear to me at all, especially with how much she is using it."

"Just because one is something, doesn't mean they love it," Evan says, looking through Sabine. She nods and sighs in a way that breaks my heart. Both of them know that so well from their past family ties.

"I'm going back to Chepstow to confront them," I say.

"Who's involved, do you know?" Sabine asks.

"Sounds like everyone."

When I say it, my breath holds in my chest.

"Is Marco involved too?" Sabine asks.

Rhydian answers, "No, he's in the dark about what has been going on. He's waiting in the house for our return." His slight smile gives me some relief that not everyone is part of this.

"Is everything we spoke about here, in this house?" I ask.

Sabine nods. "Yes. Your father's home is all but empty of treasured possessions."

Rhydian and Evan look surprised.

"What? It's time. Everyone in that town is having their fresh starts, and now, so will I. I don't want to be in that huge house all by myself." I shrug.

Evan smiles and winks at me.

Before we leave, Sabine hugs me tight. It's no longer the awkward hug from when I first met her and went with her after my father died. Instead, it's a hug from my grandmother, who I love.

CHAPTER 21

During the transport, Evan holds my shoulders, and we land in a dark shadow in the backyard. Rhydian transports inside the house as planned.

Looking at the back of my father's house, I don't feel sad like I thought I would.

"It feels foreign to be here."

"That's because you're pulled toward magick, and that's near the Lunar Falls. This is only a shell of a structure, Willow, not where your heart is anymore."

"Thank you, Evan. Unfortunately, that's not completely true. The good memories are still . . ."

"They're here. We're out of time," Evan says in a deadpan voice. He quirks his head. "It's a distraction to be here together. It's planned. I'm going to the mirror gate, don't take too long." He transports.

Tick-tock, tick-tock.

Goddess, please give me the strength to confront them.

It's dark, but the landscape lights and the eve lights from the house give shape and shadow to the grounds. There are a few birds littered throughout the yard. Dew is now crusted on the grass, and the air has a snapping chill.

I turn toward the edge of the drive. Two people are standing there. It's Lucy and Daniel.

A lightning strike happens behind me in the yard; it sizzles and charges the air. I don't turn to see it. Lucy has one hand in the air. Rhydian is in his Guardian armor.

"You've accepted your valkyrie side?" I yell.

Lucy mockingly laughs at the question. "Not all of us were born how we see ourselves, so we undergo our own metamorphosis. The Human Principality made me see. Vanessa enlightens us to your distorted goals."

There is screaming above me. When I look up, I see Emily hurdling toward me in a bubble that has her suspended in the middle with lightning crackling all around it. I use my magick and hold her with the wind. Lightning strikes the bubble, and she absorbs it and winces in pain.

"Em!"

She looks at me, and her face is tired and wary. Her eyes are wide when Daniel points off to the side of the property. There are several more people who are entering the grounds. Big guys, all muscle and height.

Lucy is staring at me as if we are strangers.

"What is this? Lucy, come to kill me?"

Lucy purses her lips and throws her arms at me to knock me back with a stiff wind. I drop Emily to the ground, and the bubble surrounding her dissolves, and the lightning returns to Lucy's chest, and she smirks. It's as if she's charged.

"What the hell, Lucy!" I yell.

Emily is not moving easily. She looks so frail. "Em? What is this?"

"For what you are!" Lucy yells back. "For what you both have done! To me!"

My heart stops in a moment. It's not what she says, but the venom of it, who I am.

"What have I done to you, Lucy?"

"Doesn't matter anymore. You are an abomination on this earth. You can't be who you are. The only way to save you is to end you."

"You're insane. Do you think you're saving me? You're killing people! This is murder, Lucy!"

"A means to an end," she says.

Her shoulders square back as she lifts her chin. She runs at me with her hands holding charges of lightning. I allow her to hit me, and she sends a solid blow across my face that turns me toward Daniel. The look on his face is pure victory. I see the hate from them and take it on as my own.

Rhydian moves so fast that I barely track him when he responds with an uppercut to Daniel's face. Cross and Marco join Rhydian, and they are engaging the five big guys that are close to us. Hits and kicks are being traded.

I turn, and with a flip of my wrist, I toss Lucy with my magick and slam her on the ground.

She throws lightning. I command it back to her, and she absorbs it. Lucy is crawling and grabbing the ground to get closer to Daniel, who is running toward her.

I am the embodiment of the Goddess. Screw her little light show.

My hands flare as I lift Daniel into the air and bind his hands in front of him. "Nice storm tonight."

"Put him down, you freak!" Lucy screams.

Daniel laughs. "It's a storm that's been coming. What since prom?"

His bound hands reach to the sky, and lightning cracks across the sky and looks like it will hit him before he throws his hands forward. It hits the corner of my father's house. A light rain follows.

Another strike of lightning nears the front of the house.

"So, having magick makes you what to these

hunters, an asset? The genocide of all magick, so you can have it all?" I ask.

"Don't," Lucy says, but she's looking at Emily.

Emily is holding her hands above her head in surrender. No threat, no action. Cross and Rhydian join us, with mud and blood down the front of their armor. Cross stands next to Emily, looking pained over her injuries.

"Emily, choose. Lucy is not innocent, and she will need to answer for what she's done. You're responsible for murder, so many have died."

"Sorry, Lucy," Emily says before looking at me. "She's gone too far down a lane that I can no longer travel or protect her from. I choose to be and am an Edayrian, a proud valkyrie, and someone who chooses magick in this world."

"Family thicker than blood? That's what you used to say. You're a fucking traitor!" Lucy screams.

Unfamiliar tears fall down Emily's thin, gaunt face. "No, you are! Aligning yourself with someone you barely know! Vanessa is twisting you and manipulating you. You allowed her to poison me and Daniel. He's controlled and hates you for it! Her goal was never you. It was Willow! Your jealously is pathetic that you would choose it over your own happiness. You murdered for it! Hell, you're okay with him torturing me and hurting me? Me—your family! Who the fuck are you?"

"What? Who?" Rhydian is in front of Lucy. He grabs her throat, and she shows her teeth in a grimace.

Quinn. Oh, my Goddess, did she kill Quinn?

"Reveal." Is the magickal command Rhydian uses. Lucy's hands light up as Cross rubs his shoulder, and when Daniel's hands light up, my lower back feels like a beacon. Each of them marked us.

"You?" Cross says.

"Yeah, but I got the prize," Daniel says, dripping with contention. Rhydian tosses Lucy in a heap near Daniel. He's still in the air, where I'm holding him.

"Did you mark Qui—?"

"Who?" Daniel says when he looks at Lucy and winks. "I mean, she's so good at the marking piece. She sure hates this group."

Rhydian looks murderous, and it pulses through me. The anger, the betrayal, the hurt and pain. They are responsible for Quinn. Daniel was with me, so she must have delivered the killing blow, along with countless others.

I thrust my hands forward and lift Lucy, twisting her in the air. Daniel drops to the ground. Emily is covering her face and buries it in Cross's chest. The pain I send to Lucy travels across her skin. She screams, and it echoes, but not over my voice.

"Did you kill Quinn?"

I pull back the pain on Lucy. Tears are streaming

down her face, and she clamps her lips shut. I repeat the question, but I see her face contort. It's all hate, and I no longer recognize her as my friend.

Lucy reaches toward him, "Daniel, help."

"How do you want me to help you? All the plans and markings you have done. Plans for Emily and Willow's deaths along with these Guardians?" He spits the words as if it tastes terrible. "I believe Rhydian's first because of Willow's love for him. Isn't it all about revenge and hate? Isn't that what we have in common? Because Lucy, no-one hates you like I do. You wanted me, right? Brought me back to this? You're weak—won't even die for your own cause. Pathetic, really."

Who is this, Daniel?

Lucy is shaking her head as if what Daniel has said is unconscionable: that he has spoken the deepest and darkest words aloud. Or maybe because her intention to kill and be rid of us all is no longer a surprise? Emily is being held by Cross. She barely has her eyes open.

Lucy has crippled her.

"I believe your words to me were whoever can mark Willow the fastest wins because everyone around her is subject to magick and is guilty of changing this world," Daniel says with a sneer. "Aren't you the one responsible for me?"

The innocent look on Lucy's face morphs into something else. She is a stranger, and I no longer have sympathy for her. She is lost with no way home. The only reason that I don't break her neck right at the moment is for Emily. Emily's face is pleading, and agony rolled into one.

Tick-tock, tick-tock.

The clock is becoming more like a secondhand and less like a minute hand. The Convergence is happening.

Rhydian looks at me as the air around us pulses. The rift in the instability of Edayri. "You know she's not worth it. She hates magick so much. Take it from her and him."

He's right. She hates it so much that Lucy shouldn't have any of it to cause harm, hex and mark people to use it with the Human Principality.

"I hate you," Lucy says to me.

"If I ever see you again, I will kill you. So run far away. You never wanted this, and now you'll never have it."

I take her magick with a curl of my fist. It's a violent rip from her body. Her scream echoes. I throw the aura that contains her magick into the sky. It disperses into a void as if it never existed.

Daniel twists himself away from us, breaking his hands apart. He directs lightning to hit my father's house. Fire booms across the roof. It's his escape. He's out of reach. When Lucy yells, he only smiles and waves to her before he touches a pin on his shirt and transports away.

"It's happening—countdown is louder. We need to leave. It was their intention to keep us here. The mirror gate at the fountain, now." I say to Cross and Rhydian. "I'm following," I say before they transport and disappear in front of me.

The fire is raging behind us. The light rain is doing nothing to put it out. My heart squeezes at the sight of it. Nothing in there is important anymore. It's a shell of an old life.

Lucy screams. The pitch of her voice is pure agony. Turning my back on her, I put my hand on Emily's shoulder and push healing magick into her.

Before I hear the scuffle, Emily sends lightning from her hand over my shoulder. I turn just in time to see Marco grab Lucy's hand, which is holding a knife, forcing her to drop it. Her stomach is charred and bloody.

Emily drops to the ground at my side.

"Goddess, what have I done?" She whimpers.

Marco lays Lucy down, then throws the knife away from them. The house continues to burn, and I hear emergency vehicles in the distance.

Lucy rolls her head away from Emily. Even in her death, she'd rather hate.

"Em. I have to leave. To stop the genocide of thousands."

Emily nods her head and slowly reaches her hand to Lucy. Marco stands at my side and puts his hand on my shoulder.

"I'm with you. Daniel can't get away with this."

I transport us to the mirror gate of Edayri in New Haven.

PART IV

The rhythm of a new moon; is uninhibited by past and future events and only measured by the present.

-The Goddess

CHAPTER 22

Someone trips over me before I fall to my knees. A crowd whisks Marco away. Too many people, it's panic. So many are rushing around and going through a holographic wave of light. It is wavering and moving. The Convergence and the collapse is underway. And not everyone has moved from the mirrored New Haven. That is really Edayri, being torn apart. Evan is pushing at one end of a holographic sheet. There is fighting all around. Guardians are ushering people from this side to the other.

"Willow, conjure magick to keep open the gate—keep the gate open." Abby is yelling at me as she holds two young toddlers and runs through where Evan is. Theon is protecting Evan and fighting off three large men.

I spy Rhydian and see him battling others in plain

clothes. The Human Principality is here to prevent us from saving as many as we can. There are so many people on the ground, unmoving. Blood is everywhere. Swords are clamoring. Cloaks, armored Guardians.

"Willow now!" Evan screams.

"What do I do?" I yell back.

"Tap into the connective magick of the realm!" He yells.

Inhaling the air, I sense the connection and the pull of magick, the coursing of my magick within to all of it outside of me. It's a tether, a source. That's it! A combo of the two, a tether of the source and my power.

"I've got it." I transport to the other side.

Tullen is helping an older person across through the gate. So many Guardians are helping as many as possible, yet so many are not going through as they fight off the Human Principality.

My magick flares. I try to lift the mirror gate through my body with all that I am. I can't seem to grasp it. Evan's hands are alight. So I form a light ball, and I attach it to the wavering sheet of this realm and lift it higher. My side rises; the holographic sheet that was collapsing is now clear. I can see through the mirror gate to New Haven which before was almost empty, is virtually full and teeming with life and color, like a technicolored dream. The magick is calling me on the other side of the mirror. Fighting is happening on that side too, but Guardians run back through to help fight back the Human Principality to get more Edayrian's across.

If we stay on this side, we will be on the side of the collapse.

Ax is near me, and he's carrying several little demon children. He runs through the gate, and several more see that it's open. They run, most of them caring for children and the elderly.

I lock my arms and my legs so that everything stays above me. I shake from pushing the gate as my muscles strain.

Tick-tock, tick-tock, tick-to—

I force my magick into my hands, command it to lift the holographic gate, and push it above my head. Evan is doing the same. It's almost as tall as the pillars of the Hallowed Hall. It's thrumming through my body and shakes me so severely that I bite my tongue and taste the iron.

Become more; you are more.

I hold steady, locking my knees as the gate pushes me to the ground. My arms are shaking. Evan is using one arm while casting with a free hand. He's moving people through the gate by force.

Daniel is near me. Eoin is blocking lightning, trying to provide cover for those running. Daniel is indiscriminately hitting as many as he can. Some stumble and keep going, but there are two who stop and fall into a heap. I pull one hand away from the gate, but it drives me down hard, and I put my hand back to push back.

You are the most powerful among them.

In her purple cloak, Sabine is using defensive magick against another woman in a black cloak who is pushing toward me. The woman in the black cloak turns, and it's Vanessa, Coral's stepmother. A Wiccan with powerful magick. But she is uncontrolled and not as experienced or as powerful as Sabine. The unpredictability of her magick is wreaking havoc. Her magick is like a whip of smoke with barbed wire. She sweeps her hands, and nearby Guardians are being struck with magick and dropping to the ground, unmoving. It must be poisonous.

Daniel kicks over a young Guardian whose face is blank.

"No!" I scream. My muscles strain at seeing his evil smile. His eyes find me, and he wipes his mouth and laughs. Then, his hand fills with lightning, and he throws it right at me. Tullen dives in front of it in one leap and falls at my feet. Ax is back through the gate, and he pulls Tullen through.

The rush of people flowing through at various transporting speeds is overwhelming. I do not move. I barely register the colors of the people all around me, but the one that gets my attention is Rhydian. His speed and grace are moving through so many. Theon, Cross and Marco are nearby, and they've made a pinch point for what seems to be the last of the people to get through. Goddess, I hope it's the last of the Edayrians.

I call to Evan in my head, *"We need to fight. She's killing people in masses. We can't let them through to those who made it. The fight needs to stay here."*

Evan responds, *"New plan, on the count of three, let it go—drop the gate. Those left we can get through."*

One, two, three.

I drop my hold on the gate and fly into the air. My muscles breathe, and the gate snaps into a smaller shape, the size of a single door. Lightning flies past me, narrowly missing me.

Daniel.

Marco jumps on his back and throws his elbow into his neck. They roll, and Rhydian grabs a weapon on the ground and throws it at him but misses. Daniel gets him with lightning on the shoulder. Marco, complete in tiger form, roars. Cross is running, his arms pumping, but I get there first.

No mercy.

There is a thrumming noise, loud and echoing. I barely register Rhydian yelling my name when I feel something slice into my shoulder and someone knocking me out of the way. I roll. I see Eoin. His eyes unmoving, his mouth slack, and a bullet hole neatly round in his forehead. Rhydian falls next to him with blood streaming from his side.

Daniel is holding a sword and a gun. With a sickly smile, he is pointing the gun at me, aiming toward my heart. Then he focuses the aim on Rhydian. He knows where to cause the most damage.

I shake uncontrollably and my scream echoes, pushing and throwing anything near us.

Be the Goddess.

My hands and thoughts are the weapons.

I pull the gun from his hands and disintegrate it with a snap of my fingers. He runs at me in full charge. I lift him over my head and scream as I twist him. He turns, lands hard, and throws lightning at me.

Laughable.

Catching it, I bend it to my will like a snake around my arm. I control it and him.

You control it all.

Daniel, for the first time, moves defensively.

"Where do you think you're going?" I twist my hands to contort his body at odd angles. His muffled noise confirms his resistance to my torture. So unrelenting at the pain I'm causing him. I feel it, the snapping of his arm, the pulling of his hip. I can rip him in two.

"I could end you quickly," I say aloud.

"What's stopping you? Do it!" He screams.

"Willow." Rhydian coughs blood from his lips. He's next to Eoin.

I've snapped the neck of the woman responsible for Mrs. Scott and my father's death. Daniel, the manipulator, deserves no less. Is he the reason Lucy changed? Or is she why he changed? They've hurt so many—Quinn. Lucy killed Quinn, but Daniel led Marco and me there for some other reason. An opportunity for mass casualties?

Rhydian is closer.

The ticking in my head is speeding up as seconds become milliseconds.

Sabine and Vanessa are in a full-on battle of magick. Evan is casting some enchantment on the gate and continues to move the few remaining Guardians and warriors to Ax, who is tossing them through, including Eoin's body.

Daniel struggles and screams. I break his leg, send his own lightning to hold him by the neck. I hear Marco roar and sense his change behind me.

Pulling at Daniel's feet, stretching him. I hate him despite my tears and my dry throat. I mourn for Daniel before the einherjar warrior they made him into. My first love who would never hurt, let alone kill, anyone.

"Why Daniel? Is there no saving you? Please . . ." Marco pleads.

"No. I should already be dead! You both know it!

So do it, Willow! End my suffering and yours because I won't stop. She won't let me."

His eyes move to Vanessa. She's controlling him.

My shoulders shake. I let go of the lightning around Daniel's neck, and it severs his head from his shoulders. I give him what he wants, a death that was his months ago. His body and head fall back to the ground, but I don't look, only the sound confirms it.

"Now, Willow!" Evan screams in my head.

Vanessa yells, watching what's left of Daniel on the ground. She turns to Sabine, all fury and rage.

I'm two steps ahead of her. I use the air to sweep all of us in transport through the closing gate. The gate wavers and closes in a big rush of air. The ground we stand on is the true realm of New Haven. It rumbles and quakes; Edayri has collapsed and is no longer.

Guardians are gathering the remaining Human Principality fighters and tying them up. There are so many faces watching me as they hold on to each other.

"Where do you think you're going?" A loud voice booms over the crowd.

I turn to Vanessa, the leader of the Human Principality. She uses her poisonous black line of smoke in a magickal a whip, but before it touches people, I push them out of reach. Then, using the surrounding air, I vault us above everyone, so that they are out of the reach of her magick.

"Others will take my place. You won't win, not in Terra, not even here." She seethes. Her words like venom from her dark red lips.

"Maybe."

Evan's faint voice is in my ear. His words a plan to end the Human Principality—to track it back.

I guide Vanessa's magick around her like a snake. The smoke constricts her, and she struggles. "But you and the Human Principality will no longer have the magick born of the Goddess to persecute others."

"You're nothing but an over-privileged brat."

I radiate the glow from my skin, and it hovers all around me. The magick crown lifts high over my head. The gasps below me don't deter my attention.

"I'm the Goddess and the Wiccan Queen. And you're nothing more than a narcissistic murder whose time has ended."

I look at Evan. His hands make various patterns and shapes with light and magick, and Sabine is at his side.

"Do you have it?" I ask.

"We do," Sabine replies.

I pull the magick from Vanessa and throw it to Evan and guide us both to the ground.

"What did you do?" Vanessa's face is full of fury.

"Magickal signatures, of course. Now we can

disband your work completely. You've led us to all of it. Every cell you've got around the globe," Sabine says.

Evan has the magick signatures of the gate and from Vanessa, all contained in a clear magical box. The contents are a mixture of light and smoke. An organized storm of destruction. Ax and Aren, the chairpersons from the legion council, approach us.

"You are in the custody of the legion council for charges of treason and genocide of its people," Aren says.

Ax slaps binding cuffs on Vanessa and then throws a stone to the ground that opens in bright light and envelopes her before it closes in on itself, muffling out her scream and rage. Ax picks up the stone and tosses it a few times in front of his face.

"So tempting to throw this and forget it," his deep voice says.

"There needs to be justice served for all that she's done to Edayrians," I reply.

Ax's grin reveals his fangs in what some consider a scary smile, but I only know it as his. General Thaxam, who is a noble demon and fierce protector of equality for Edayrians.

"You know, I agree." He winks.

I nod and face Sabine and Evan. Aren has the box and is walking from us. Most of the spectators have dispersed throughout the Hallowed Hall grounds and gardens. The Guardians are grouped together, and healers are checking each one of them out. Those lying on the ground are being covered in sheets.

I spy Eoin being draped and find myself staring at the sheet. I don't know how, but I sense something lift in my heart. A vision of Eoin and Quinn together. Is this real or my mind playing tricks on me, because I see them in an embrace. The Elysian fields, Heaven or Valhalla. The comfort wraps me like a warm blanket to know Eoin and Quinn are together, just as I picture my father and mother are together.

CHAPTER 23

S abine is grinning, her eyes soft. "Oh, sweetheart, you've saved us. You are truly the embodiment of the Goddess."

"Nah, she is the Goddess," Evan says.

"I should have gotten here faster. Done more."

My heart breaks at my confession. Now I know how Evan feels.

Time heals.

"Time does heal," Evan says.

"Did you hear her in my mind?" I ask.

He nods.

I hear a few gasps and hushed tones. Sabine leans into me and says, "Willow, it's the Goddess and the Horned God. Um . . ."

I turn and see the shimmery silk of her roman-like robe and teal cloak floating about the ground, with her hair swept up on her neck in ringlet curls. She is the Goddess. The Horned God is next to her, holding her hand. His large horns on his head sweep back and twist, similar to his long auburn hair. His chest is bare and muscled; his pants are loose white linen.

Evan and I approach the floating Goddess and Horned God. I am a wreck. Dirt and mud—tear streaks down my face. I smile weakly at the two of them. So many died today. Why couldn't they intervene?

"You know why," the Goddess replies.

Do I? Maybe I do? I'm not too fond of it. To be omnipotent of creation, only to let us succeed or fail on our own. It is our choices after all.

"I don't see failure here. I see a Goddess Wiccan Queen who saved her people. Although the cost was high, it was not without a victory. Here is a new realm not of my making but of—"

"Yours." The Horned God walks over to us.

Evan smiles at me.

Arizona?

Yes.

His voice is barely a whisper in my mind, but I knew the answer before he said it.

Evan claps the Horned God on his back as if they are old friends, and they turn away from us, whispering. The Goddess chuckles, watching Evan and the

Horned God. I don't feel like I could do that with the Goddess. It seems inappropriate.

Her smile is gentle, and her head tilts to answer me without saying a word.

"We should speak more. My fault for not preparing you for what all that you will be to them." She waves her hand toward those watching us.

I don't want to question her because she is regal and omnipotent. Edayrians revere and fear her. She is the reason for Wiccan creation. Being chosen by her worries me. I'm not without flaws.

She turns to me and lays her hands on my shoulders.

"Being adored and worshiped is something that can inflate one's ego toward defining perfection. My mistake was of wanting perfection instead of realizing that perfection is a construct of flaws while learning to be better. Let's say it took a lot more time for me to understand and appreciate."

"Okay . . . how do I fit into this?"

"For one, you're allowing me and my love to return to our celestial place together. You now hold my abilities within your being. So that you may lead and mold the Wiccan rule into a modern, tolerant age."

Can I do that?

"You already have, by bringing cultures and beings together within the legion council that you established. For one so young, you are more experienced than you know."

I feel the heat of my cheeks with her compliment.

Evan and the Horned God turn to where the Goddess and I are standing. Like a couple of old pals, they are very comfortable with each other. I bend my head in somewhat of an awkward bow to the Horned God.

His baritone laugh puts me at ease. "Willow, I think it's I who should bow to you. I need no formality. It's a pleasure to meet you finally."

Looking into his eyes, they are dark and holographic. His eyes move like a star constellation. The wrinkles around his eyes stretch upward as he smiles, and it puts me at ease despite his towering figure.

"It's nice to meet you too," I respond.

"So, this is your niece." The Horned God looks at Evan. "I see the family resemblance. She got all the best parts." Evan laughs in response. "I'm sorry to see that it will separate you both, but it is an honorable duty."

"I'm sorry, it will separate us? I don't think I understand."

The Goddess says nothing aloud.

You won't be alone.

Evan looks at the ground and kicks at the gravel pathway. He doesn't meet my eyes. He motions to the

Horned God and says, "Would you mind giving us a few minutes? I haven't explained."

When both the Goddess in the Horned God nod, Evan leads me over to the side of the Hallowed Hall stairs.

"Evan? Just tell me, rip the band-aid off."

Evan smiles. "One of us will need to stay in New Haven, and the other will need to stay in the Terra realm. Ripped off band-aid."

"Is life all about loss?"

I'm sure my response was not the one he was looking for, holding my arms and tears falling. Evan hugs me, and I hug him back. My mother's brother, my uncle, who meant more to me in the last year than I ever thought he would. He is a connection to the family I've lost, and now I will lose him.

"No. All loss brings new beginnings. Try to relish in those opportunities. Because if you don't, take it from a broken man, living in the past will devour you. I know my sister and your father—they would never want that for you."

I nod my head into his chest, still hugging him. "Does this have to happen now? Or do we have time?"

Evan closes his eyes and inhales the air as if to feel a response. I sense nothing but clean, crisp air on a chilly morning. "We have a few days. We must honor the dead and the living before transportation connections are closed."

"Why would they close?" I ask. I already know the answer, the grounding of magick and the flow of the realms.

"It's safer and more stable this way. You know that the Goddess and Horned God, when together, create instability. As we take up the mantel . . . Therefore, it must be this way."

I recall Tullen teaching me the history of the Goddess. We walk back to the Goddess and the Horned God. I spy Rhydian off to the side, not far with a watchful eye on everything we're doing. He is speaking with Ax, Marco, and Cross.

"So, now that you both have taken to your roles, we shall leave you to all of it. We will no longer be its keeper," the Horned Gods says.

"Wait, like ever?" I look at Evan.

"Okay, I thought that was understood." Evan shrugs his shoulders. "Me casa, es us casa?" Evan smiles.

All I can do is shake my head. Maybe I saw this coming? The things I can do when I only concentrate and think them through, I can make happen with little practice. The Goddess did crown me, but I didn't understand that I would take up in her stead. Does that mean—can I remove them—?

"You have a question?" She asks.

I hesitate to ask, but she may be the only one to address the blood vow. Rhydian, I don't feel the ache because he is near. Instead, it's the weight of removing something that pulled us apart to begin with. To right the wrong that I forced upon him. The blood vow he took to protect me, that I helped him break to remove his father's control.

"If it wouldn't offend, I would like to ask what can be done regarding Rhydian's blood vow to me? The blood vow is broken because I forced his hand. We both ache in pain from the connection when we are apart. Can the blood vow be removed? I want us both to have free will to choose, but this failure of protection in the vow is something we—I'd like to remove."

The Goddess smiles and looks from the Horned God to Rhydian, who is still to far to hear us. "The blood vow was quite vain, but I appreciated its loyalty at the time. Willow Sola Warrington, you are the Goddess and you can absolve it."

"Is there a special spell or—"

"Only the will to do so, with concentrated intention. You can do literally, anything."

I pause before putting my hand in front of my chest and pull the vow's threads. A pale, pink light pulses in front of my eyes and disappears. I watch it do the same in front of Rhydian without his awareness. The blood vow is no more.

The missing ache lifts and is replaced with a pounding heart of free will and uncertainty. The Goddess, smiles knowingly.

Both the Goddess and the Horned God disappear before my eyes.

Be well and Blessed Be.

Evan speaks with the legion council and transporting is cleared for all, the rifts are no more. A mass funeral will take place in two days, a day before the closure between realms. The once crowd of people is now down to a handful.

I meet Rhydian near the fountain.

Guardians and others are transporting to various Terra locations.

Rhydian is holding my hands and looking into my eyes. "Tullen is making a full recovery. He will meet you in Arizona. Cross is going to Chepstow to ensure that is all buttoned up; and he'll be with Emily to tell her what happened to Daniel."

Is Rhydian not coming to Arizona? I shake my thoughts and focus on Emily. It crosses my mind that since Emily helped create Daniel as an einherjar warrior, she may already be aware of what has happened.

"You're no longer tied to me. As the Goddess, the blood vow is absolved. I guess, if you had let me finish what I started in the cave, I could have technically done it then."

His face is unreadable when he replies, "Okay."

I pull back my hands from his. "I know that so much about me is—well, Queen, Goddess. It's a lot.

The good news is that we are both free of the pain when we are apart, Rhydian."

He is still, his eyes roaming over my face.

"Is it easier for me to stay or is it easier for me to go?" He asks.

Stay. Stay. Please stay. I hope beyond saying the words.

Instead, I ask, "I know what my answer is, but what is yours?"

"This is not a straightforward decision." he replies, his voice deep and discouraging.

Oh Goddess, my heart is in my throat. It's like we are back at MacKinnon manor. The blood vow broken, he's broken, or is it me? I can't tell.

Don't leave.

I close my eyes, waiting for him to say he can't stay. It replays in my mind when he turned away from me and left. Lost in my thoughts, I barely register a hand that gently touches the side of my face. It's his hand and I lean into it. He's saying goodbye. We are back to where we were, but it's his choice. I will not impose my wants on him.

I could. It would be wrong.

My tears threaten to fall.

"Willow, look at me," he whispers.

I want to, but I can't.

His lips gently touch my eyelids and my forehead.

I savor the feather touches because they could be our last.

"I'm staying, Willow. I'm staying. You are the most sacred person to me."

My tears fall. He's staying, and it's his choice. There is no influence, nothing is compelling him beyond his own mind, his own heart. Rhydian drops to one knee. "I commit myself to your service, if you'll have my blood vow—"

"No. Stop." I shake my head.

His confusion looks unsteady with the emotions across his face.

With tears flooding my eyes, I continue, "What's sacred is our choices and freewill, if I've learned anything over the last year. I'm beyond honored, but how about we date first?"

His smile is wide, and his chuckle comes in a burst as he stands. "Absolutely."

I lean into him, and our lips connect.

CHAPTER 24

Flanked by Rhydian and Cross, I'm incognito to those around us. I touch the marble square that rises high into the sky with the names of the Edayrians lost. Commander Eoin and Quinn. I also think of the names not on this monument, Daniel and Lucy. I've cried so much that my tears hold, but I wear the sadness in my mind and my body. The only thing that really makes it less horrible is Rhydian's hug around my shoulders.

I step back, and Cross moves forward and touches Quinn and Eoin's names before leaving them. One straight tear falls from the man who shows no fear of anything or anyone.

They held the mass funeral on the New Hallowed Hall grounds, as the first Convergence Remembrance Day. All that has happened with the collapse of Edayri will never be forgotten. The legion council has a refugee fund among the families that were displaced. Democratic ideals are finally coming together to help one another within New Haven. Although I sense some still harbor prejudice against each other, more have an open mind toward working together. Evan made an odd but sweet speech about magick and its home.

"I'm getting an ear comm that Evan would like to speak with you," Rhydian whispers in my ear. I nod back to him and ask where. He points toward a bench where Evan is sitting. "I won't be far behind," Rhydian says.

"So protective." I grin.

"Well, when I need protection, I want the best." He kisses my temple.

I sit next to Evan on the bench, remembering the time when he transported us to France. When I learned about the Emissaries, and my parents' involvement for equality. I feel as if I have aged five years since then, not physically, but certainly mentally.

"So, what do you know?" Evan asks.

I lean into him and bump his shoulder playfully. "Coral is with her father back in Massachusetts. I can collect on insurance money for the house in Chepstow. And I believe the refugee fund will use it well."

Evan looks up at the sky. "Don't tell me what I already know, tell me what *you* know."

"That time will heal? Although saying it feels trite, and I want to hit someone when I hear it. I know I won't see you, and I'm sad about that."

Evan nods his head and says, "Same, I am sad too. You forget our connection, and that we can speak to each other anytime." Evan lightly touches my temple. "Just like how I would speak to Nuala, your mother. We can do the same."

My excitement turns from mourning this day to small celebration. I can still to talk with him.

"Yeah?"

He nods his head and laughs. It's infectious, and I join him. The sound is almost foreign to my ears, but it feels right.

"So, I guess I should leave now. I heard from a certain celestial there might be an opening between realms. Maybe? Have you seen into the future?"

Evan shakes his head. Only riddles and subtext he'll reveal, which I'll never completely understand. But I hold him tight in one last hug before rejoining Rhydian and Cross to go through the portal, back to Arizona.

"Just one more thing." Evan whispers in my ear, "In four years' time, the portal will open. I will see you in white, hand in hand, walking down an aisle of a church, and it will be my pure honor." He kisses the top of my head and leaves me a little stunned.

Rhydian approaches and holds out his hand.

"What? Another riddle?"

"I get the impression the realms will open every so often."

"Oh yeah? Any idea when?"

"In four years." I answer and can't stop the blush that I feel creep across my cheeks.

"A lot can happen in four years."

"How about just one day at a time?"

"Absolutely." Rhydian is squinting and assessing me, but doesn't press for more.

Cross claps his hand onto Rhydian's back, and Tullen comes over and hugs my side. We walk through the portal and transport to our new home in Sedona, Arizona.

CHAPTER 25

The morning alarm is jolting, and yet again, I roll and slap the snooze button. Holding my hand on the alarm, I then press the off button. It's the final alert that if I don't get up, I will be late. I toss the covers over my head, open my eyes, and breathe in the five minutes before I rise and shine.

The tiled floor is cold on my feet as I shuffle across the large room toward the bathroom. Duke stretches one leg out as I walk by him. He is hitting the snooze button one more time.

I'm jealous of my dog.

The water from the shower is a welcome start to a new day in my new life. I dry off and study myself in the mirror. The familiar hum rises to the surface and the light patterns of magick dance all over my skin like a full-body tattoo. So much has happened in the little over two years since I discovered my Wiccan and Royal heritage. Time doesn't erase the loss and pain, but grieving is a process where the edges wear away.

In the closet, I pick out my clothes and walk into my room. Lastly, I sit on the bed and tie the laces of my purple chucks. It feels a little like déjà vu from high school, but I'm starting my first year in college. Although a little later, it's my start. Duke and I make our way downstairs.

Walking toward the familiar voices, I pause at the wall, hidden just enough to spy.

Emily and Cross are laughing easily. A sound that makes me smile. Despite the losses they've suffered, they have found solace in each other. Emily buried Lucy, and they folded her death into the arson of my house. We attended Daniel's burial as a soldier killed in a rogue training exercise. It was hard to face his parents and sister, knowing his death occurred well before that day. Coral and her father have moved on as well, and purposefully, we don't keep in touch. Although the organization of the Human Principality is gone, the risk is not one either of us will take.

The legion council has members here and in New Haven. Guardians are being reestablished with protection and policing mandates to ensure magickal beings blend into Terra and ensure that we are not taking advantage of Terra with magick. Most are scared of using magick, so for now, it's been peaceful. A new commander was named, and Rhydian seems to like him. So much has changed and yet—

"Can you believe it? I'm a Sun Devil now?" Emily says. She sings a tune as she moves somewhere in the kitchen.

Cross, without skipping a beat, responds, "Oh the devil part, I can believe for ya."

Tullen surprises me when his hand lands on my shoulder.

"Whatca you doing out here? We've got a schedule to keep. First day and all."

"Yes, professor." I reply, grinning, and follow him into the kitchen.

"That's adjunct professor." Tullen smiles and straightens his collar. "I'm excited about this, because I'll get to work toward my PhD in theology and mythology."

"So, how did you get that job again?" Cross asks.

He is chiding Tullen. It's been an ongoing joke that Tullen may have influenced the department head with either magick or flirtation, because Tullen didn't quite fit the job description requirements in education, but he certainly knows his stuff.

Rhydian is at the round kitchen table, his eyes focused on the phone in his palm. But not for long. He gravitates toward me, his eyes, his smile, and I can't help but return the look.

"Good morning, beautiful," Rhydian says. He greets me at the coffee machine, Fancy, before kissing my temple. "Missed you on the run today."

"I wouldn't say I missed it," I reply.

Duke pushes up against my leg, then Rhydian's before Rhydian pets his head. "So a run, huh? You weren't being lazy sleeping in, traitor." I waggle his ears, and it feels like Duke smiles before I hand him his morning treat.

This is my life and my people.

We all live in this house on the mountain in Arizona with Sabine and several others. It's close enough to the cavern where the Lunar Falls is that we can monitor when the New Haven portal might open or if there is a shift. So far, there's been none, which has been a blessing. The only part that is missing from this bliss is that my family is no longer with me, but then again, looking around, I have the family that chooses me, and I choose them. Tullen in his slacks, hair pulled into a messy lower bun with his full red beard. Cross all muscles and strength towering over the slim Emily, who could drag him around by his pinkie literally. Rhydian, his ocean eyes no longer storming but calm, his dimple threatening to show with his smirk.

"What are you thinking?" Rhydian asks. He holds me at my waist. His smile lightens any downtrodden mood that could lurk in.

I wrap my hands around his neck. "That I'm one lucky girl."

"Are you ready to start the rest of your life?" He asks.

"I'm ready."

The End

AUTHOR'S NOTE

Book reviews matter. If you enjoyed SACRED. Please leave a review where you buy and/or review books, so that this book can be discovered by readers just like you. This support helps me continue publishing. Thank you for your support.

ACKNOWLEDGMENTS

To my family and friends, thank you for the love and support. Especially to Butch, Allison, and Danielle. You give it all meaning.

My editor, Spencer Hamilton, for your push and encouragement to revisit this series and helping me finish it. It's a wrap!

Shout out to the Rebel Authors who I adore, and our illustrious Mother of Villains - Sacha Black, thank you for everything. The fun and the push in all the right ways.

To Writer's Atelier and my Write Gym mates, especially our leader and coach Racquel Henry, thank you for the ongoing unwavering support, write-ins, and accountability check-in's.

To the readers, thank you for the support and joining the journey with me, the ride isn't over, it's just getting started.

ABOUT THE AUTHOR

C. M. Newell is an award-winning YA fantasy author, receiving the 2016 New Apple Fantasy Award for her debut novel Magick in The Unwanted Series.

C. M. is a lover of all things fantasy and fairytale, especially the twisted ones. She loves to write strong female characters who don't fall victim to circumstance but instead rise above. She prefers a world where a princess can save herself.

Originally from Tennessee and a nomad from various states and countries, C. M. now calls home to sunny Florida with her family.